WOMEN'S BEACH CLUB

GETAWAY BAY RESORT ROMANCE, BOOK 3

ELANA JOHNSON

Copyright © 2021 by Elana Johnson

All rights reserved.

No part of this book may be reproduced in any form or by any electronic or mechanical means, including information storage and retrieval systems, without written permission from the author, except for the use of brief quotations in a book review.

ISBN-13: 978-1-63876-012-2

ONE

TYLER RIGBY PUSHED his foot against the ground, giving his hammock another gentle sway. The afternoon hours were some of the longest, and while he should've been used to them after six years, he still wasn't.

It was moments like this that he thought maybe he should get a job. The idea only stayed for a breath, a fleeting moment. But it had been plaguing him for a few months now.

"Maybe after Christmas," he said to the golden retriever. "Yeah, Lazy Bones?" He pushed the hammock again. "Maybe after Christmas." Which was still a couple of months away too.

Not that Tyler kept track of time anymore. He had no reason to, other than he liked eating eggs for breakfast and going somewhere for dinner. And no one had their dinner menu on at three o'clock in the afternoon.

The waves of the bay lapped at the shore a hundred

yards away, and Tyler focused on them as his phone buzzed against his bare chest.

His brother, Wayne, who still lived in New York City, still ran the multi-billion-dollar online poker company they'd founded together almost a decade ago, still kept in touch on the daily.

Tyler had trained his brother not to talk to him about poker, the company, or anything business related. He had financial advisors for that, and speaking with them on a quarterly basis was horrific enough.

Wayne's message was a picture of him and his two kids, and it said, *It's Darius's birthday* underneath it.

Tyler snapped to attention. One thing about having a huge fortune at his disposal and countless hours on his hands was that he sometimes forgot what day it was. Darius was one of only two nephews, and the boy would only turn six once.

So Tyler called the toy store in New York City, and got someone to deliver a set of the toy cars his nephew liked so much. That done, he decided he could head inside his modest home and get ready for dinner.

After all, he hadn't showered yet, believing the best hours for showering were between three and five p.m. As he stepped out of the bathtub in his one bedroom house on the beach, something clunked and then a soft scrape followed.

The mail. He looked forward to the mail every day, as it simply gave him something to look forward to. He'd thought more and more often lately that if he had a girlfriend, he'd have something else—something fun—to anticipate.

He wrapped a towel around his waist and went to collect that day's excitement. He thumbed through the envelopes, finally pulling a cream-colored one out of the stack. It had elegant script on the front, reading *Mister Tyler Rigby* and ending with his beachside address on Getaway Bay.

He opened the letter, wondering what it could be. Probably another invitation to some fundraiser. Though he wanted to maintain a low profile on the big island of Hawaii, everyone seemed to know he was loaded.

He pulled out an equally eggshell-colored piece of paper, already dreading what it said on it. His attention perked up when he realized it was an invitation to the gala celebrating the completion of the new children's wing of the Bay Hospital. Since he'd made a sizeable donation—really, without him, the wing wouldn't have been possible—he and a guest were invited to the fancy-pants dinner next weekend.

Something else to look forward to. As soon as he thought it, he tossed the pages to the kitchen counter. He'd be expected to take someone. The last ritzy dinner party he'd attended alone, he'd gotten quite the tongue-lashing from the media.

Problem was, he didn't have a significant other. He hadn't done it to hurt anyone, show anyone up, or boast about his wealth, as the article had claimed.

Lazy Bones whined, and Tyler went to work filling the dog's water bowl and dishing up more dog food. With the retriever lapping at the water, Tyler snatched his phone from the counter. Within seconds, he had Marshall Robison on the line.

"Dude, I need a date to a charity event," he said.

"I'm not really your type," Marshall said.

Tyler could practically see him bent over a stack of paperwork at his desk. Marshall owned the largest pineapple plantation on the island, and they were both members of the Hawaii Nine-0 club, an informal organization for the men and women who had nine zeroes in their bank accounts.

"Very funny," Tyler said. "I'm just wondering…you used to have a lot of different women go to events with you. Where…well, where did you find them?"

"Oh, that's easy," Marshall said. "You just ask someone you already know. Tell them explicitly that you're not looking for a relationship. It's not a date. You'll buy them a fancy dress, and they'll hang on your arm, and get a free meal, and pose for the pictures. Most women like that."

Tyler couldn't think of a single person he knew who even wanted a fancy dress. Or knew how to pose.

"Want me to set you up with someone?" Marshall asked.

That idea was even more horrifying than going alone. He'd be spending hours with this woman, and he'd like to be able to enjoy the money he spent, maybe have a decent conversation. Okay, so maybe he should just be looking for someone to ask. If they wanted to think it was a date, well, would that be so bad?

Only one person came to mind, and he wasn't sure if

she'd even remember him. He hadn't spoken to her in months, and he was surprised the beach yoga instructor hadn't called the police on him for stalking with a dog. Could he help it if Lazy Bones liked her stretch of the beach the best? Could he help it if he liked watching her hold difficult yoga poses with ease?

No, he couldn't help either of those things.

"Ty?" Marshall asked.

No matter how many times Tyler had told Marshall not to call him that, he still did. The man had a fixation on nicknames.

"I'm good," Tyler said. "Thanks, *Marsh*." He hung up, a low chuckle in the back of his throat. When he came out of the bedroom after getting dressed, Lazy Bones stood by the back door, a Frisbee hanging loosely in his mouth.

"You want to go throw?" Tyler took the toy from his dog and headed back out to the beach. If there was one thing he loved doing to occupy all his free time, it was working with, training, and playing with Lazy Bones.

His feet drank up the warmth in the sand, though it wasn't as hot in October as it was over the summer. As he completed the easy motions of throwing the Frisbee and treating Bones, his mind ran through possible ways to approach the beautiful yoga instructor and not make a fool of himself.

An hour later, he still didn't have any good ideas, but it was close enough to dinnertime to wander down the beach and find something to eat. He rounded the curve in the bay and drank in the sight of Getaway Bay before him.

At the pinnacle of the bay sat Sweet Breeze, the new

luxury hotel that had just celebrated its one-year anniversary. Fisher DuPont owned and operated the hotel, and he was also a member of the Hawaii Nine-0 club.

Several stands and huts dotted the bay, and he could get tacos, fruity drinks or sodas, fish sandwiches, anything with spam on it, popcorn, and the best grilled pineapple on the island right here. Tyler loved eating on the beach, and while he sometimes wondered what he was doing with his life, he loved living the way he did.

After so many years in the spotlight, with the designer suits, and the fancy haircuts, and never being able to leave the house without a security detail, he'd come to Hawaii—to Getaway Bay—to well, get away.

He didn't own more than one suit now, and most days he didn't even put on a shirt.

His eyes wandered down the beach, to the dozens of vacationers in Sweet Breeze's private beach—and his gaze stalled.

The cute yoga instructor with brown hair streaked with blonde.

He'd met her over the summer, and yeah, he'd thought her fit and fun and probably fabulous. He wasn't really sure, as he'd never worked up the courage to talk to her past saying, "Sorry about that," when Bones had knocked his Frisbee into the woman's beach yoga class. He'd never even gotten her name.

Perhaps it was time to do exactly that.

With new purpose in his stride, he stopped at the seafood stand first and Two Coconuts, the drink hut, second. Properly fed and hydrated, he approached the yoga class, which was just getting out. He'd seen the woman plenty of times, and he'd seen the cup from Two Coconuts by her mat as well. He carried a second one with him, having done a bit of espionage at the drink stand.

He stopped several feet away and watched as she toweled herself off. She had well-defined muscles in her arms and legs, a trim waist, and all the right curves in all the right places.

She caught his eye and froze. Tyler lifted the cup in what he hoped was a universal gesture of *I got this for you so you'll go to a fancy event with me next weekend, and hey, I'll buy you a dress if you don't have one.*

She actually glanced over her shoulder, as if she expected someone else to be standing there. Someone else he wanted to talk to. A pin of guilt pricked his heart. His many hours at the poker table had taught him to read people really well. Sometimes it was actually a curse, because he instinctively knew he'd hurt this woman by not talking to her when he should have

She took a tentative step toward him, and he moved too. "Hey," he said. "So, uh, I'm Tyler." He extended the drink toward her.

She lifted the one she already had, and a wall of foolishness hit him. "I know who you are," she said, a note of disdain in her voice.

"Oh, yeah?"

"Yeah." He lifted the drink to his own lips and sucked. Pure sugar coated his mouth, and he spat the offending liquid out. It stained the sand blue, and he stared at it in horror. "What is this stuff?"

"Blue raspberry," she said, cocking one hip in a way that made his heart pound a little faster. And not because he was striking out and wouldn't have a date to the gala. But because, as he had for months, he found her so, so attractive.

That smattering of freckles on her face. The streaks of blonde in her light brown hair. Those blue-green eyes, the same color as the bay.

Lazy Bones trotted right up to her and began to sniff in all the wrong places. Tyler tried to get between the two of them. "Bones," he chastised. "Stop it."

"Oh, he's fine." She bent and patted Lazy Bones, the smile on her face the first genuine gesture he'd seen since approaching. Bones soaked up the attention as if Tyler never gave the dog a good scrub. He grinned at the woman as if telling Tyler he'd been knocking his Frisbee in to this woman's yoga class for a reason.

"What's your name?" he asked.

She straightened, and Lazy Bones went back to the sniffing. Her eyes blazed, and for one, two, three terrible moments, he thought she'd stalk off. Instead she asked, "Did you ask Mo at the drink stand what I like?"

She'd find out anyway, so Tyler said, "No. Her name was Leilani."

"Why?"

"I have—I want—I *need* a date." He was so rusty when it came to women, he might as well leave now. Send in his own scathing article to the paper and take a selfie of him shirtless and unshowered for the photo. He tried to get Bones away from her, though he thought she smelled pretty amazing too. Like suntan lotion, and sand, and sun, and sweat.

"Is that an invitation to go out with you?" She plucked the drink cup from his hand and removed the straw. She handed it back to him and put her straw in before taking a great big drink. She finished with a long, "Ahhhh, that's good," and a cocked eyebrow.

He stared at her and then started laughing. "Okay, I deserve that."

"You really do." She made no move to give him the drink back. No problem. He'd bought it for her.

"So I donated a bunch of money to the children's wing at the hospital, and they're having their celebratory gala." Tyler watched her for any tells, anything that would indicate how she felt about what he was saying. She remained wooden, her emotions carefully hidden behind a mask. She'd be very good at poker.

"It'll be boring, and it's a black tie event," he continued. "*Very* stuffy. Very non-yoga. But I'm wondering if maybe you'd like to come with me."

He put on his poker face too, and though it was out of practice, it allowed him to make it through several seconds of silence. Was she ever going to answer?

He cocked his hip too. Two could play this game, and he was pretty sure his time at a poker table meant he could outwait her.

TWO

EVERY CELL in Tawny Loveless's body tingled. The beachy billionaire was standing in front of her, asking her out.

Asking *her* out.

He gazed back evenly at her, and Stacey's label for him —the bashful billionaire—seemed a perfect fit. She claimed that was why he hadn't made a move with Tawny yet. Apparently Tyler was friends with Fisher, and Fisher had said he didn't get out much.

Except to hospital galas, obviously.

Tawny desperately wanted to say yes, but she wanted this guy to work for it. To know that she'd been right there all these months while he tossed the perfect Frisbee to his adorable dog. The dog who wouldn't stop sniffing her. She pushed against Bones's big head, and the dog backed up a little. Maybe he didn't get out much either and all these new smells were driving him wild. Still. Mister Sniffington needed to chill.

"I never got your name," Tyler said, nudging the dog back with his leg again.

Of course he hadn't. She knew all about him, and he didn't even know her name. Classic. Tawny tried not to let it bother her; she wasn't the international poker celebrity who'd sold his company to his brother for over six billion dollars.

"Tawny," she said, deciding not to keep him waiting any longer. "Tawny Loveless. I work for your friend, Fisher." She indicated the hotel.

"Oh, you know Fisher?"

"He's dating my best friend, so." Tawny shrugged like she was hanging out with billionaires every day of the week. As if. Maybe in her dreams, if she actually dreamt. No, she hadn't been blessed with nighttime dreams that left her warm and woozy when she woke. She had to do all of her dreaming during the day, which made her imaginations more like fantasies. And maybe a few of them had featured the long-haired beach bum with billions concealed in his bank accounts. And his big dog too.

She lifted her cup and drank, sure just because he had a lot of money didn't mean he could read her thoughts.

He appraised her, and his bright blue eyes sharp and intelligent now. Okay, so maybe he could read more than the average person. "What do you think about the gala?" he asked. "No strings attached."

Oh, but Tawny wanted strings. Strings that turned into rings, and rings that held diamonds.

Slow down, sister, she told herself. First, she'd go out with him.

"I'll have to check my yoga schedule." She lifted her chin, determined not to squeal and jump into his arms. She couldn't come across too eager. That tactic had never served her well, and she'd been making some new rules for herself when it came to men.

Rule Number One: Make them work for it.

Rule Two: Don't act desperate.

Tyler lifted his phone to his ear, his eyes never leaving hers. "Yeah, hi, can you transfer me to Owen? It's Tyler Rigby."

"What are you doing?" Tawny asked.

He tilted the phone down from his mouth. "Calling to check on your yoga schedule."

She lunged for his phone, but he stepped back and held it out of her reach. A chuckle vibrated from his mouth, and it was as deep and wonderful as Tawny had imagined.

"Yes, Owen, I need to know when Tawny Loveless is working next weekend."

"I have it on my calendar," she growled. Her blood streamed through her veins, too hot and too fast.

"Just in the morning on Saturday? Great, thanks so much, Owen." He lowered his phone, a drop-dead gorgeous smile on his face. "You're free that night."

She slicked her loose hairs off her forehead and faced him again. "Maybe I already have a date."

"Do you?"

No, she didn't, unless she counted her fluffy white dog. "Fine. I don't have a date."

"You could." He shifted his feet in the sand, almost like it was too hot for him to keep standing there.

She sipped her drink, glad he'd brought her a cold one. "All right." She held out her hand and flapped her fingers.

"What?"

"Give me your phone."

He handed it over without question, and she added her number to it. "Text me the details."

"Do you have a dress? It's black tie, remember?"

She stepped into him, and placed her palm flat against his chest. Yeah, okay, so he spent some time working out too. "Oh, honey, when I said text me the details, I meant the details of when we'll meet so you can help me get ready for this...black tie event." She patted his chest, maybe once more than she should've.

"I wouldn't wait long," she said as she walked away. "I might need to order something from the mainland." Tawny felt his eyes on her, but she refused to look back.

"How about tonight?" he called after her.

Tawny spun and walked backward, hoping with everything in her that she wouldn't trip in the loose sand. "I'll check my schedule." Then she turned and left him standing there, chuckling, on the beach.

———

Have you had time to check your schedule yet?

Tawny smiled at the text on her phone from an unknown number. She saved Tyler in her contacts and re-read the words, hearing them said in a playful tone. She'd barely left the beach when the message came in, so she ducked behind a tree and looked back toward where they'd been talking.

Tyler still stood there, his dog now lying at his feet, his sniffing needs apparently satisfied. When she didn't respond, he cast a long look in her direction but Tawny felt certain he couldn't see her. Sure enough, he bent and picked up a blue Frisbee and threw it, the dog taking off after it and then trotting back to his master.

What time were you thinking? she typed out. *I need to shower and I have a few things to take care of.* Not entirely true, but she didn't want him to think her only options on a Friday night after work was a shower and her TV while she painted and cut fabric.

My schedule is completely open.

Have you eaten?

Tell me what you want, and I'll meet you there.

Tawny smiled at her phone, her stomach warring with itself. She definitely needed to eat, but doing so in front of him didn't sound like a good idea.

"You can eat in front of a man," she told herself. She continued along the trees, down the beach to her house. It was a long walk, but she was tired of riding her bicycle to the hotel. Sterling had bought a rack just for her, but she just needed a break from that scene. She'd tried a few dates with the valet, because he was cute, polite, and employed. Her requirements for a date were getting shorter and shorter, and Sterling had been kind and charming. He was good-looking. But there had simply been zero spark between them—at least for her.

And seeing Sterling day after day, and that bike rack he'd bought just for her...well, it felt like she was rubbing something into his wounds she didn't need to rub.

By the time she got home, she'd decided where she wanted to eat. *The Noodle House, seven-thirty*, she texted him. *And can you pick me up? I don't exactly have a car.*

Sure. See you soon.

Giddiness accompanied Tawny as she burst into her beach house and exclaimed to her pup, "I have a date with the bashful billionaire!" She laughed and dropped her duffle bag by the front door. She bypassed the purple T-shirt she'd been planning to decorate and then cut into strips that night. She made all her own workout shirts, and she'd learned numerous ways to tie them into different patterns so she didn't get ridiculous tan lines. Getting paid to work out on the beach had its benefits, but that wasn't one of them.

She showered, dressed, and dried her hair before checking her phone again. Tyler had texted again, asking for her address.

She sent it to him and then decided her outfit was all wrong. She dialed Esther, and blurted, "The handsome beach guy finally asked me out."

"Tyler?"

"Yes, Tyler." She giggled as she pulled her sundress over her head. "We're going out tonight, and I have no idea what to wear."

"What would you normally wear?"

Tawny paused. The dress. "So the opposite of a flirty dress." She pulled a pair of white shorts out of her dresser and paired them with a blue and white striped top. Made more of T-shirt fabric than anything else, it was casual attire, *nothing* like what she'd wear on a first date with a man she'd kept one eye on for the past four months.

"Listen," Esther said. "Just be you, okay? I know you're doing things different or have new rules or whatever. But you are you. That doesn't change just because he's handsome and rich."

"Says the woman who already has the handsome, rich boyfriend." Tawny managed to keep the bite out of her tone. Mostly. She jumped when a knock sounded on her door. "He's here." She wasn't sure why she was whispering.

"Beach tomorrow, all the details," Esther said. "I'll text everyone."

"Gotta go."

"Good luck!" Esther's parting words spurred Tawny to find a pair of sandals while she called, "Coming!"

She arrived at the door a bit out of breath to find him wearing a pair of blue shorts that could've been a swimming suit. He wore a gray T-shirt that looked brand new, and wow, he made casual wear look like a tuxedo.

His long hair had been pulled back, and it looked wet along the top where he'd combed it. He hadn't shaved, and his seven-thirty-shadow made her throat dry.

"Sorry, I'm a bit behind," she said. But she did not want to invite him in. She kept her house in a state of messy-chic, with piles stacked in specific places. She knew what was in every stack, and she had a method to her madness she didn't particularly feel like explaining to him on the first date.

"Did I rush you?" he asked.

"No," she assured him. "Just stood in the shower a little longer than normal." She rotated her shoulders. "I've been working this one shoulder a little too hard lately."

"Yeah?" He looked at it and his hand twitched like he might give her a massage right there in her doorway. "You should have Fisher's spa people fix you up."

"Yeah," she said evasively. "I should."

"I've heard they're good."

"Oh? You get tight from all the surfing?" She plucked her purse from the hook by the door and pushed closer into his personal space until he backed out onto the porch.

"Surfing is actually very athletic," he said. "So yeah. I might indulge in a little heat therapy from time to time."

Tawny smiled at him, thinking *it must be nice to have time and money to do that.*

A hint of sourness filled her mouth, but she swallowed it away. Fisher would probably let her have spa appointments for free. He was generous with his staff and his low turnover rate proved they liked him.

"So what brought you to Hawaii?" she asked.

He cut her a look out of the side of his eye. "You've read the Internet."

"Surface stuff," she said, which may have been giving away too much. She wanted more than surface stuff, and that didn't sound like no strings attached. "You don't have to tell me." She moved toward his car, a sporty little number that came in the brightest red possible.

"I came because my mother died and I wanted some-where beautiful and happy to wake up to each morning." She spoke the words without a single hiccup, but the weight of living in a world without her mom hit her right beneath the ribs. She kept the smile on her face and added, "Isn't Getaway Bay the most beautiful and happiest place on earth?"

"It sure is." He stepped around the car and opened the passenger door for her. He blocked her way, though, and said, "I'm sorry about your mom."

She looked right into his eyes, finding genuine warmth there. "Thank you. Me too."

He moved and she slid into the car. When he joined her, he said, "Both of my parents still live in New York City. Well, Queens."

"Do you see them often?"

"No. But I talk to them a lot. My brother too. He's older." His jaw twitched, and Tawny felt like he had more to say but he didn't.

And while Tawny had a million more questions for him, she let the ride go by in silence, because it felt nice, comfortable, new, and casual. And she really needed some-thing new and casual right now, even if it was only for a week. Even if he only needed her to hang on his arm for an event. Even if it had taken that to get him to come over and talk to her when she'd been ogling him for months.

She swallowed back the doubt and reminded herself that at least she'd get the best noodles on the island and a new dress out of this, even if he really did mean *no strings attached*.

THREE

TYLER LIKED noodles as much as the next guy, but to listen Tawny talk about them, they were the nectar of the gods. He liked her exuberance, the good vibes she put off, and the way her white shorts ended high on her long, tan legs.

"So you're kind of a celebrity," she said once they'd gotten their food and found a table on the patio. An awning covered the whole thing in shade, and Tyler reached for his fork to eat the Japanese snow pea noodle bowl he'd ordered on her recommendation.

He took a bite, the saltiness of the sauce a nice compliment to the sweet snow peas. "I'm not a celebrity," he finally said.

Tawny didn't miss much though she kept her eyes on her own bowl of noodles. "But you do need someone to go with you to the gala." She looked up. "Why?"

So maybe she didn't read the papers or the web as often as he'd assumed. He couldn't see a reason not to tell her, so he said, "Last time I went alone, I got blasted in the media."

"Hm." Her eyebrows went up and she stirred her noodles around. "Only celebrities get blasted for what they do or don't do."

Tyler couldn't argue with that, so he didn't. "So the event will be mingling at first. Drinks and some of those little appetizers." He hated mingling, and he'd been to way too many parties to enjoy hors d'oeuvres anymore. If he'd eaten one salmon canapé, he'd eaten them all.

"Then there will be a fancy dinner. Sometimes there's dancing." He lifted his water glass to his lips and drank. "And a speech. There's always a speech." He hoped they wouldn't call him up on stage. In fact, he made a mental note to call the event organizer and ask them not to. He didn't need that scene, even if he had a date this time.

"How long is the whole thing from beginning to end?" she asked.

"Oh, hours." He exhaled like he'd already been, already suffered through the night. "Probably about four. We can make a graceful exit by eleven."

"And I need a fancy dress."

"Something suitable for a cruise ship, or say, a wedding banquet. I can pay for it."

Tawny lifted those intoxicating eyes to his. "That would be great. My yoga salary doesn't really pay well enough for sequins." She smiled at him and indicated his noodles. "You don't like them?"

He picked up his fork, not having the heart to tell her he'd eaten fish tacos on the beach before approaching her. "They're great." A sense of pride filled him that he was out with a woman, talking to her, and that he was actually enjoying himself.

He wondered what had taken him so long to talk to this woman who'd caught his eye months ago. Ducking his head, he knew why. If he started a relationship with a woman—especially one like Tawny Loveless—there would be questions to answer. Secrets to reveal. And his very private life to expose.

But she already knew he was a billionaire, so at least that was out of the way. And she seemed like she'd be fun to spend time with, even if the event didn't appeal to him.

"I came to Getaway Bay to get away," he said, scooping up another bite of noodles, bean sprouts, and shredded carrots.

"Do you still play poker?"

"No." He barked the word and immediately felt bad. "Sorry, I...no, I don't play." He didn't do anything in his life that he used to. He'd left it all behind. The adoring fans. The scads of women. The prestige. The ten-thousand-square-foot house.

For a while there, he'd adored his life. Thought he'd gotten everything he'd ever wanted. But he hadn't realized how shallow he'd become, and he couldn't remember exactly when he'd become someone he didn't recognize.

He looked up and flashed her a smile that felt awkward on his face. "I'll come pick you up, and there will be people who'll want to take our picture together."

She nodded like she'd been through this numerous times. "I'll practice my smile." She gave him one and he thought it was already pretty darn perfect.

"Shoes," he blurted. "Anything you need." He reached into the outside pocket of his shorts and slid a credit card toward her. "I've got a purchase watch on this card. I'll see everything you buy, and from where." He barely knew her, but the watch provided some sense of security. He had to reply to the watch notification before the charge would be approved. So he'd be tied to his phone while she made her purchases, but if she tried to use his card for more than a dress, shoes, maybe some makeup, he'd know and be able to refuse the transaction.

Tawny stared at the diamond card, which was clear and sparkly. Then she swept her palm over it and it disappeared into her tiny purse. "Thank you."

"It's just one night," he said, not sure why he was reiterating that. Probably because he didn't want her to feel obligated to meet with him again before next week, or that she needed to know anything about him for this event.

"One night," she echoed. "Right." Tyler finished his noodles and drove her home. Sitting in her driveway, with her little white dog perched in the front window, he said, "Thanks for doing this."

"Sure. It'll be fun." She glanced at him. "Thanks for dinner."

"Sure. It was fun." He looked at her, and the moment between them lengthened. He wasn't sure what he was feeling, because he hadn't been interested in anyone in a long time. And the last woman had stolen his heart and never given it back. So while it thudded in his chest, the cracks in it threatened to give out. Apparently surfing in Hawaii hadn't healed him as completely as he'd hoped.

She blinked, breaking the moment between them. Clearing her throat, she reached for the door handle. "Thank you, Tyler." And she was out of the car before he could fully process how gently she'd said his name, how much emotion the two syllables carried. She arrived at the front door, turned and waved before going in, before he realized he wanted to hear her say his name over and over again.

———

Tyler paid Mo to take a drink to Tawny after her evening classes, and she texted him every time. He was much better through messaging than in person, because he could think through the answers, type and re-type them until he was sure they sounded the way he wanted them to.

After years of quick thinking and showing zero emotion, Tyler liked having more time to formulate responses without having to worry about who was watching him.

"Who are you texting?" Marshall sat down beside him at The Palm Palace, where the Nine-0 club was meeting that night.

"No one." Tyler flipped his phone over though it buzzed and he was dying to see what Tawny had said. The Palace wasn't Tyler's favorite place, because the music was always so loud and the food could only be classified as mediocre.

But the meetings moved, and they were really more about casual discussions and friendship, so Tyler went along with whatever. He hadn't called a meeting since the inception of the group, so he couldn't complain. If he had initiated a meeting, it would've been on the beach, and most of these guys would stand out like a sore thumb in their expensive suits and shiny loafers.

Tonight, Marshall wore more casual clothes, something he'd been doing more and more of since he's started dating his driver, Esther. His polo still looked like it was hand-woven from the finest silks, and his khakis were just a little too perfectly pressed.

"Who'd you ask to the gala?" Marshall asked next.

"Some woman from the beach." He kept the emotion out of his voice, thankfully. "What about you? Are you going?"

Marshall didn't hide his status or money, and everyone knew he had it anyway. "Not this time. I don't have anything to do with the hospital."

Surprising, as the Robison's had something to do with everything on the islands. Tyler acknowledged Fisher as he wove toward them, along with Lawrence, Jasper, and Lexie.

Fisher had called this meeting, and he wasted no time getting down to business. "So we've got some potential new members," he said, waving away the waitress. "A pair of sisters stayed at Sweet Breeze last week, and they told me they're relocating to the bay area. Sure enough, they're here again, and they've got a house out by the western parks."

"What do they do?" Marshall picked up one of the folders Fisher had put on the table. He flipped through it and handed it to Tyler. He didn't care about what was inside. Fisher was nothing if not thorough, and he prepared little dossiers on prospective new members of this club he cared so much about.

"Online clothing." Marshall looked at Tyler. "That's up your alley."

"Lotta money to be made on the Internet," Tyler acknowledged, opening the folder. "Oh, Clothia.com. Yeah, I know them. Big campus in New Jersey, they do a lot of selling through their website, and were the first to have an app for clothing purchases too."

"Is it really a billion-dollar industry?" Lawrence settled next to Fisher with a glass of clear liquid in his hand.

"Fashion?" Fisher nodded. "Of course. Think about how much you pay for your clothes."

"The fashion industry does over a trillion dollars in revenue worldwide," Tyler said as if reciting from an online encyclopedia. His photographic memory had helped him in more ways than one during his poker career, and once he read something it was very hard to forget.

Marshall tapped and swiped. "Clothia is worth two-point-two billion dollars."

"So they qualify," Fisher said, looking around, clearly asking but without phrasing his statement as a question.

Lexie looked through the other folder. "Who's this?"

"Gabriella Rossi," Fisher said, leaning over to look.

"She owns a controlling stake of her family's cruise ship enterprise."

"She's on the island now?" Lexie looked up from the brunette in the photo.

"I've been informed that she is, yes." Fisher wouldn't say more than that. How he found people who wanted to fly under the radar, Tyler wasn't sure.

"Have you talked to her?" Lexie asked.

"I haven't spoken to any of them." Fisher gazed at the others. "I'm wondering if we think we might like more members?"

"Sure," Marshall said. "We're pretty low-key, and it's nice to have friends that don't want something from you."

"I can talk to Gabriella," Lexie said. "We used to run in the same circles."

Fisher quirked an eyebrow at that, and Tyler couldn't help wondering how a cruise ship heiress and the majority shareholder of the biggest mutual fund company in the world would ever run in the same circles.

But Tyler, as the world's youngest professional poker world champion, shouldn't have ever been associated with a top real estate developer and a generational pineapple plantation owner.

But he was. And he was glad he was.

They spoke for a few more minutes about increasing their ranks, and then Fisher leaned closer to Tyler. "I heard you're going out with Tawny Loveless."

"Yeah. I mean, no. I mean, we're going to the hospital gala so I don't get crucified in the press again."

"Oh, is that all?" Fisher spoke with a note of uncertainty in his voice, and Tyler remembered the way his heart had reacted to Tawny at dinner.

"Yeah," he said again. "That's all." Even if he found her beautiful and easy to talk to, he'd told her no strings attached and he wasn't going to expect more than that.

FOUR

TAWNY EYED her last hope to find a dress before tomorrow night's gala. And even if she did, the chances that it wouldn't need to be altered would be a miracle. Desperation surged inside her, and she turned to look at her best friend.

Stacey gathered her red hair into her battle mode up-do. "All right. This is it."

"What if they don't have anything?" She and Stacey had been to every dress shop on the island—well, besides this one—and they'd even gone over to Maui yesterday. This shop looked like it used to be a soup kitchen, as there was no sign above the double glass doors set in the long strip of businesses.

But Stacey had heard from a good source that this was *the* place to find a dress. Tawny had her doubts. After all, why hadn't either of them heard of it before?

"Don't give up yet," Stacey said as she unbuckled. She met Tawny's eye. "Positive thoughts."

Tawny had enjoyed herself immensely that week, what with all the evening texting with Tyler, the shopping with Stacey during the day, and the idea of going to a real-live gala like she was a princess. She'd had more fun in her yoga classes, and her tips had increased by fifty percent. Yes, this had been a very good week.

"And hey, if there's nothing here, there was that green one. It would be okay."

Tawny nodded, but she didn't want okay. She wanted spectacular. This was a *charity gala*. And she was going with a *billionaire*.

She squinted when she got out of the car though she wore sunglasses. The glass mirrored back the parking lot, and she couldn't see inside the doors. Stacey went first while Tawny inhaled deliberately and prayed this would really be a high-end dress shop and that they'd have something in her size.

She'd started out the week insisting on wearing something blue to the gala. But after the first three shops had proven difficult to even find something suitable, her requirements had slipped. She was down to the right size, and even that could be worked with.

Stacey gasped, and Tawny hurried into the shop behind her. "What?"

"Look at this place."

A magical dress land spread out before Tawny's eyes, and she hitched her glasses up onto her head. "Wow." The garments closest to the door were white, clearly trying to capture the brides-to-be as they walked in. But the colors and styles extended as the racks went on.

It was a tiny shop, only extending about thirty feet back, but Tawny's spirits soared. She could find something here.

"Hello, ladies," a woman said with a Japanese accent. "What you looking for?"

Stacey indicated Tawny, who'd already started leafing through a rack to her right. "She needs a dress for the hospital gala tomorrow night."

The shorter woman appraised Tawny, her gaze sharp. "I have something for you. You come."

Tawny exchanged a glance with Stacey before following the woman past several racks of dresses that held things Tawny would like.

"You size six, yes?" She turned and looked at Tawny again. "Maybe four. I can alter." She pushed this dress aside, and then that one, finally pulling out a royal blue dress and holding it up. "This one."

Tawny fell in love at first sight, the lace and beadwork on the bodice the most beautiful thing she'd ever seen. The dress would skim the floor, and she'd need shoes too.

The woman shook the dress. "Take. Take. I find shoe."

Stacey took the hanger and said, "I guess we try on over here." A row of curtains hung in the back corner and Tawny sort of floated toward them, the image of that blue dress so wonderful she couldn't believe it.

Stacey helped her into the dress, which had no straps and left her feeling exposed. Beautiful, but exposed. "I guess I wear about this much on the beach while I work out," she said.

"Totally," Stacey said. "And what's the point of working out so much if you can't wear a dress like this every once in a while?" She stood back and brushed her hand down Tawny's back as if trying to make the fabric lay flat. "This is the one."

"It's a little tight," Tawny said, wondering if the woman had given her a four to begin with.

"She said she can alter it."

"By tomorrow night?"

The woman opened the curtain, no announcement or knock necessary, obviously. "Ohhh." She hummed and moved around Tawny, touching and pinching the fabric. "This nice." She held up a pair of gold heels and said, "Step in."

With the shoes on the ground, Tawny followed her directions and stared at herself in the mirror. She imagined herself with her hair curled and flowing around her shoulders, her makeup stylishly done, maybe a pair of crystal earrings with a bracelet to match….

"I'll take all of it," she said, a swell of warmth filling her from top to bottom. "You can maybe let the dress out a little?"

"Out here." The woman touched her stomach. "Maybe in here?" Her fingers flitted along the sides of Tawny's breasts.

She nodded. "Yes, please. And I need it for tomorrow night."

"I finish by noon," the woman said. "Okay?"

"Okay," both Stacey and Tawny said at the same time. Once the woman had gone, Tawny dissolved into giggles. She felt flushed and chilled at the same time, and she wiped her forehead as Stacey unzipped her in the back.

"I can't believe we found this place."

"I can't believe you're going out with the bashful billionaire," Stacey retorted. "It's about time."

It was about time, and Tawny couldn't help smiling at herself in the mirror. Now, she just needed to turn this no strings attached gala date into more than a one-time thing. She paused her train of thought before it could pick up speed.

She always thought like this, always got ahead of herself, always fell faster and harder for the man she was with than he did for her.

Not this time, she promised herself. This time, she was doing everything the opposite of her natural instinct. And that meant that tomorrow's gala would be her and Tyler's last date. She couldn't—wouldn't—hope for more. Wouldn't plan on it. Wouldn't worry about it.

———

Knocking echoed through her house just as Stacey slipped the bracelet on Tawny's wrist. "You're perfect." She beamed at her. "Go have the time of your life."

Tawny gave Stacey a quick hug, a silent thank you for the hours of work she'd put in on Tawny's hair, her makeup, and for bringing over a few pieces of her grandmother's expensive jewelry.

A hint of missing accompanied her steps as she moved through the house to answer the door. At times like this, she'd love to have her mother with her, helping her get ready for a fancy party and talking about the handsome man on the other side of the door.

She opened the door to greet him, and they both stood there staring at one another. He wore a freshly pressed tuxedo, the white of his shirt almost blinding it was so pure. His hair had been cut, shaved on the sides but left long on top. He'd slicked it back again, and he hadn't shaved in days.

He looked every bit the part of a caring, generous billionaire, and her heart beat wildly as she struggled to remember how to breathe.

Without speaking, he stepped across the threshold of her house and put both hands on her waist, drawing her right into his chest where she could smell the citrusy, sandalwood, beachy quality of his skin.

Finally remembering how, she breathed in deep as her eyes drifted closed in bliss. The moment felt like a wizard had put them under a spell, and he broke it by stepping back and saying, "Wow."

That was all. One word. And Tawny had no idea what the wow was about. The chaste embrace that still had her reeling? Her dress, makeup, and gold shoes?

He offered her his arm and said, "Shall we?" like he was a real-life fairy tale prince. She slipped her hand through the crook of his elbow and let him lead her out to the sidewalk. Instead of a horse-drawn carriage in her driveway, a long, black limousine sat there, with a driver as impeccably dressed as Tyler standing near the back door.

"Sir," he said as he opened the door. "Madam."

Tawny had literally never been called madam before, and a smile sprang to her face. Her stomach felt like someone had injected a bunch of angry bees into it, but as she got in the car and situated her dress, she began to calm. She obviously looked the part. Just because she taught yoga for a living didn't mean she didn't belong on Tyler's arm.

He joined her in the backseat, immediately taking her hand into his. Tawny was so out of her element, but she still felt sure that holding hands in the back of a limo was more than no strings attached.

"Something to drink?" he offered, his voice low and filled with an emotion Tawny couldn't identify.

"No, thank you," she said, sure she wouldn't be eating much of anything tonight. Not only were her guts a little too tight, but she worried over spilling something on the beautiful—and expensive—dress.

You didn't pay for it, her mind whispered and then it went blank as Tyler leaned over and inhaled her hair. It felt like an intimate gesture, something a man would do to his girlfriend because he couldn't get enough of her.

"I can see my money was well-spent. You are gorgeous." He adjusted his hand in hers, making the grip slightly tighter. She liked that he called *her* gorgeous, not said that she *looked* gorgeous. There was a distinct difference, and Tawny could've melted.

"It took all week to find this," she said. "But she got it altered in time, so it all worked out."

"Aiko is excellent," he said. "I'm glad you found her."

Tawny turned toward him in surprise. "You know her?"

"She is the best seamstress on the island."

"You could've pointed me in her direction on Monday." Tawny shook her head even as a smile touched her lips. "Saved me a lot of wasted hours, not to mention the panic."

Tyler blinked at her, his blue eyes kind, soft. How had he been a ruthless poker player? Certainly not with a gaze like the one he wore now. "I assumed you'd know the shops on the island."

"Oh? So you pegged me for a shopaholic, is that it?" She infused just the right amount of teasing into her voice, because a grin graced his strong mouth.

"Do you like to shop?"

"I actually make all my own yoga shirts," she said. "From simple T-shirts and fabric paint."

"Yes, the one you had on this morning was quite…stringy."

A flash of lightning went through Tawny. "You saw my shirt this morning?" It had been stringy. Mostly strings, in fact, as she'd cut the shirt into long strips and then pulled and twisted them before tying them all back together into a knotty, stringy pattern. Her bright pink bra top had shown beneath it, just the way Tawny liked.

He cleared his throat. "Lazy Bones wanted to chase a ball."

"Way down on my stretch of the beach." She felt like her eyes were sparkling, she was flirting so easily with him. "That dog. I don't think he's as lazy as you think he is."

Tyler chuckled. "That he is not."

The limo eased to a stop, and Tawny's muscles tightened again.

"It'll be fine," he said. "Just be your charming self." He, however, removed his hand from hers and fiddled with his bowtie and then tucked his phone into his breast pocket. "I'll go first. They'll take a lot of pictures. Wait for Hank to indicate you should get out." He nodded at her like he'd just completed a business transaction, and she instantly missed the easy, casual side of him.

The door opened, and flashes were already popping as the sun had set at least a half an hour ago. Shouts met her ears, and she clutched her hands together, hoping she could put on the show Tyler required.

At least a minute went by before Hank dropped his hand and said, "Your turn, Miss."

Tawny scooted to the edge of the seat and made sure both of her gold heels were on solid ground before putting her hand in his and pushing herself to standing. Hank passed her to Tyler, who secured her against his side like she belonged there.

And for the first time in a long time, Tawny felt like she'd finally found someone worth getting to know, worth spending her time with.

He only kept her in front of the reporters for a few seconds, and then they moved up the sidewalk that had been cordoned off with long, black ropes. He paused every time someone called his name, and a walk that should've taken thirty seconds took ten minutes.

By the time Tyler opened the door and ushered her inside, Tawny felt like her face would crack from all the smiling. A rush filled her, though, and she half giggled, half exhaled as she leaned into Tyler.

"That was exhilarating," she said.

"You think so?"

"Yeah." She peered at him. He was so calm, so cool. She felt like a jackhammer had been inserted into her core and was going full speed. "You've done this more times than me, obviously."

His jaw twitched and he looked toward the ballroom where dozens of other people had already gathered. "More times than I can count."

Tawny didn't like the dark note to his voice, and she slipped her hand into his, hoping to make that surfer boy return. She liked him a whole lot more than the stuffy billionaire in the tux, though he also carried sexiness in the very set of his shoulders.

"Well, let's go get some of those appetizers you promised. I can't wait to try the canapés."

That made him crack a smile, as he'd texted her about how if he'd eaten one party hor d'ouerve, he'd eaten them all. Tawny, on the other hand, had never really consumed anything in one bite besides a handful of popcorn. On the cruise ship where she'd worked, she did massages and taught water aerobics. The parties with the platters of puff pastries were out of her league and not included in her pay.

So when the first waitress appeared with a tiny meat-ball on a toothpick, she took two. "Mm." The one-bite idea was genius. Nothing to spill. Nothing to worry about.

Until she turned and saw Omar Velasquez enter the ballroom. Her stomach recoiled against the meatballs she'd eaten, and the room went white for a moment.

What in the world was he doing here? And how could she get him to leave her alone?

FIVE

TYLER SENSED a change in Tawny and he instinctively edged closer to her, though he already stood too close to be considered casual. She hadn't minded the hand-holding though. Or the way he'd practically wrapped himself around her at her front door.

He had no idea what he was doing, and he'd been acting on instinct since showing up at her beachside bungalow.

But she turned back to him with pure panic in her beautiful eyes. "I need you to do something for me," she said, her lips barely moving.

"What?"

"That man over there." She glanced over her shoulder before whipping back to him. "Oh, no. He's seen me." She looked like she might cry. "He's coming over. Can you do me a favor?"

"Sure." Tyler wasn't quite sure what she was talking

about, but he did spy a tall yet stocky man approaching them. He had the dark skin of a Hawaiian, but he wasn't from the islands. His dark eyes saw everything, and Tawny spun back to him, her fingers lacing through Tyler's as she did.

"Tawny," he said, his voice smooth but accented. He lifted her free hand to his lips, but Tawny held as still as a statue, stiffer than Tyler had ever seen her. She practically ripped her hand away from him, and Tyler's male need to protect her kicked into high gear.

"Tawny, darling," he said, his own voice as smooth as melted chocolate. "Who is this?"

She met his eye, an edge of panic still in hers. He hoped he could communicate that he was on her side with a quick look, but he wasn't sure she'd gotten the message.

She swallowed and said, "This is Omar Velasquez. He owns an empire of avocado farms in Mexico."

"Mexico, huh?" Tyler focused on the Hispanic man. "What are you doing here?"

Omar regarded him coolly, and Tyler didn't like the sharpness in the man's gaze. "I have two operations here, so I come from time to time."

"No, I meant at this hospital gala." Tyler could be cool too. Could be cruel, actually. He felt himself slipping into his poker persona, and he struggled to pull himself out of it. He hated how easy it was to go back to that person, to calculate every move someone made and use that to predict what they might do next.

"I am invited to many things," he said, switching his attention back to Tawny. "What are you doing here?"

"Tyler donated to the new children's wing," she said, her voice a bit too high. Tyler didn't move a muscle, and Omar didn't either. He clearly had experience dealing with high-pressure situations, whereas Tawny did not.

"I'm here with him," she continued, her chin lifting and her voice settling to normal. "We're engaged, Omar." She leaned forward the slightest bit while Tyler tried to figure out what had just happened. "To be married."

That got a reaction from Omar, whose gaze flew back to Tyler, anger and jealousy and a dozen other unpleasant emotions storming across his face now. Tyler secured his poker face into place, determined not to show this man that this engagement was as new to him as it was to Omar.

"To be married?" A woman put her hand through Tyler's free arm, and he turned to face the event organizer and hospital public relations manager. Paula practically purred her next words in his ear. "Is this why you called to make sure I wouldn't make a big deal out of your appearance?"

She looked at Tawny and practically ate her up. A lesser woman would've wilted under all the scrutiny, but Tawny stood straight and tall, her hand in his not too tight, her face open and still a bit afraid.

"Yes," he said stiffly, leaning a bit closer. "And we'd like a table away from this gentleman, please."

Paula focused on Omar next, and she moved her hand from Tyler's arm to his, saying, "Omar, you look fabulous. Let me show you where you're sitting." She swept him away, though he cast a long, lethal look back to Tawny and Tyler.

The anxiety in Tyler's muscles deflated, and he sagged against the wall. "Wow," he said for the second time that night, this time for a completely different reason than earlier.

"I'm so sorry," Tawny said. "I didn't know what to say." She cast a quick glance to where Paula was still towing Omar away from them. "He's my ex-boyfriend. Well, he wanted me to marry him, and I had to leave Cancun to get away from him. Then he followed me here, and I haven't seen him in months, but he's relentless. I thought if, maybe if…."

Tyler shook his head and held up his hand. "I need a minute to think." He wasn't sure what he didn't understand, only that she was talking so fast, and he just needed her to stop. A cool breeze touched his face, and he zeroed in on the balcony doors that had just been opened. "Let's go outside."

He snagged a flute of champagne from a tray as he passed, knowing he wouldn't drink the fruity alcohol. But it looked the part if he carried it, so he'd do that. As he left behind the stuffiness of the ballroom, he had a sinking feeling he'd be doing a lot of pretending and fulfilling a part in the coming days.

Because "Engaged?" came out of his mouth as soon as he'd reached the railing and made sure he and Tawny were isolated from the rest of the party goers.

"It just came out," she said. "I didn't want him to think we were, you know, a one-time thing." She wrung her hands for several seconds before planting both palms on the railing in front of her.

The ocean in front of them continued rolling in, then out, despite Tyler feeling like the entire earth had been knocked off its axis.

"Why would it matter if we were a one-time thing, or dating, or engaged?" After all, she'd skipped a lot of steps.

She sighed and leaned into the railing, her own gaze on the waves. "He told me when he followed me here that he would never stop pursuing me. Not until I married someone else." She sounded absolutely miserable, and Tyler really disliked that. He'd worked hard to make sure this night would be magical for her. Well, he'd booked Hank and the limo, dry cleaned his best tux, and made that call to Paula. Still, it was more than Tyler normally did in a whole week, so he felt like he'd at least tried.

"You're afraid of him," Tyler said.

"Yes."

"Have you filed a complaint with the police?"

"He doesn't…." She exhaled violently. "He's very well acquainted with the law. He never does anything beyond the scope of the law. He's just…scary, and relentless, and… I'm sorry." She twisted toward him, her beautiful face filled with anxiety and her eyes glassy with tears. "I'm sorry."

Everything inside Tyler melted. "It's fine, Tawny." He gathered her into his arms and they stood, watching the waves, each lost inside their own thoughts, until the announcement was made that dinner would begin in five minutes.

He had no idea what to do with a fiancée, fake or not. She wasn't wearing a ring, and Omar hadn't demanded to see it. Once back inside the ballroom, he found Paula standing at one of the front tables, gesturing for him to come sit up there.

So he put on the poker face again and led Tawny through the maze of tables to the one where Paula wanted him. "Forgive me," she whispered as he sat down, and Tyler's stomach fell to the floor.

She moved to the mic and officially began the festivities. Waiters appeared with food, and Tyler only had a moment to lean over to Tawny and whisper, "She's going to call us up on stage later. Get your game face on."

The panic and terror coursing through her eyes wasn't the game face Tyler had been imagining, but he got drawn into a conversation with the Japanese businessman on his right and had to play his part too.

The dinner dishes disappeared, and he put his head together with Tawny as strawberry cheesecake and other assorted desserts made an appearance. "I called and asked her not to call me up on stage, but now that she's learned we're engaged, she has to do it."

"Why?" Tawny whispered.

Tyler smiled like he was having a fun, flirty conversation with his girlfriend. Until Omar, that was exactly how this night had felt. He'd liked it. Had been trying to figure out how to see Tawny again even though he'd said there would be no strings attached.

"She's a huge gossip," Tyler said, gently brushing a strand of Tawny's hair off her face. Their eyes locked, and while she looked anxious still, that powerful pulse that existed between them roared to life too. "This is big news for her," he said, his whisper a bit too breathy.

If Tawny noticed, she didn't indicate as much. "We can break up later," she said. "Any time you want. No big deal."

Tyler nodded, though he hadn't even been thinking about breaking up. Quite the opposite, in fact. "We'll probably need to be together for a few weeks after this," he said, suddenly glad she'd invented this engagement. Now he didn't have to figure out how to ask her out again.

She agreed, tucking her hand into his. "I'm sorry," she said again, and he really wished she'd stop apologizing. "I hope this doesn't make your life too difficult."

"Tawny, I surf every morning. Throw a Frisbee to my dog about lunchtime, and then chill in the hammock until I can justify it's time to go to dinner." He met her eye again, something hot burning through him now. "This isn't going to make any of that harder."

Gratitude painted her expression, and she leaned into him. "Thank you. Hopefully, Omar will only be on the island for a couple of weeks. Then we can go our separate ways."

Tyler reached way down deep for his courage, the kind he'd needed to walk away from his lucrative career in professional poker, the stuff he'd relied on when he'd approached Wayne and told him to make an offer on Tyler's half of the online empire they'd built together.

"About that," he started. "I was thinking about—"

"So let's bring him up! Tyler Rigby, get up here with your fiancée!"

He spun toward the stage, where Paula wore an exuberant smile, not a stitch of regret anywhere to be found.

"Show time," he mumbled as he stood. He buttoned his suit coat to thunderous applause and extended his hand to help Tawny find her footing in those tall heels. With her hand secure in his, he started for the steps. A quick glance at her showed a very able actress, and another rush of affection for this new addition to his life flowed through him.

———

Hours later, he finally made it behind the tinted glass of the limousine, the interviews over, the questions done, the event finished. It was much later than eleven o'clock, the time he'd promised Tawny they could make a tactful exit. She hadn't complained at all, but stood at his side and said a few words when asked a direct question.

He leaned back into the seat and loosened his bowtie as another sigh leaked from his mouth. He'd never been so exhausted. Of course, he hadn't had to be so on in a long time. Talking and smiling and being so politically perfect was a far cry from paddling out to a good wave or rocking to the symphony of wind in the hammock.

"And to think I used to do that constantly," he murmured.

Tawny responded by tucking herself into his side and saying, "You were brilliant. There won't be any negative articles about you this time."

Achievement unlocked, he thought, too tired to respond. He managed to walk Tawny to her door and give her a hug that lingered maybe a few seconds too long. He wanted to kiss her, but the idea had entered his head about two blocks from her house, and he was nowhere near prepared to make that move.

They'd left the reporters behind miles ago, so he didn't have to worry about keeping up appearances. Still, he wanted his first kiss with her to be authentic and private. He would not do it for show, which meant he better find a way to get it done before he had to.

But it wasn't gonna happen tonight, and she gave him a soft smile and slipped behind closed doors, leaving him to head home to his house alone.

Alone.

He'd been alone for six years. In so many ways, he loved his independence. He ate what he liked, got up when he wanted, did whatever tickled his fancy that day. But in other ways, like entering a silent house with only a single light burning in the small kitchen, he acknowledged that he'd like someone to share his life with.

So though it was late, and they'd just spent hours together, Tyler pulled out his phone and sent Tawny a text. *Thank you for going with me. You made an unbearable event*

He paused, trying to find the right word. He had feelings for Tawny, and he didn't think he'd been too shy about showing them. But now, he didn't want to give too much away. Why it mattered, he wasn't sure.

Everyone out there thought they were engaged.

So he finished his text with the word *fun* and sent it.

She didn't respond before he got his luxury clothes off and collapsed into bed.

He woke several hours later, the sun streaming through his blinds, and his phone screaming out a call. "Yeah?" he answered without looking at the caller ID.

"You're engaged?" His mother's voice practically reached through the phone lines and choked him.

He sat up, his head pounding as the events from last night zoomed through his mind.

"Tyler David Rigby," she said, pulling out the middle name. All the way from Queens, he could feel her wrath. "You start talking right this second. Who is Tawny Loveless and why am I reading about you and her for the first time on the Internet?"

SIX

TAWNY ROLLED over the following morning, a soft, marshmallowy feeling in her bones. Last night had been a roller coaster of feelings, but once dinner had started and the engagement had been announced, it was just like acting. She'd grown up doing community theater and high school drama, and she'd thought she'd done a pretty decent job last night.

Today, though, she needed to get down to business.

She had a late-morning yoga class and then she was free for the rest of the day. So she reached for her phone to text Tyler. She saw he'd messaged last night, and she smiled at his gratitude. He was so different than what she'd been imagining these past few months.

Yes, he was tall and handsome. Rich. But he was kind too. Thoughtful. Sensitive. But powerful when he needed to be. Charming as if he didn't even have to try. He was almost too good to be true, and she wondered what secrets he'd left behind in New York City when he'd come to Getaway Bay.

We should probably get some facts straight. How we met, how long we've been dating. That kind of thing.

She sent the message and went to shower for her class. She got ready and ate a protein bar for breakfast, constantly checking her phone. Tyler had not responded. He'd said he was up at dawn to surf, but he was also laid back and probably didn't have a strict routine either.

So she put the unanswered text from her mind and headed to her beach yoga class. She didn't know where Tyler lived, and she wouldn't show up unannounced even if she did. No, the old Tawny would've done that, and she wasn't going down that path anymore.

With a sinking feeling in her chest, she realized the old Tawny would've done exactly what she'd done that morning: Text Tyler about getting together again so they could perpetuate their fake engagement.

She groaned. "Shouldn't have done that," she muttered to herself as she spread her mat on the warming sand. She should've waited for him to contact her. After all, he was the one who would have to deal with the press, not her. He was the one who needed the right facts.

But she hadn't asked him out. She'd simply said they should get some details of their relationship in place. *Nothing wrong with that*, she told herself.

Her phone chimed, but she couldn't get to it as a larger than normal group of women appeared and Tawny set about helping them get ready for the class to begin. Fifteen minutes in, her phone started ringing and wouldn't stop.

As soon as one call went to voice mail, another one would fill the air.

Tawny finally silenced her phone, wanting to chuck it into the ocean. When the entire Women's Beach Club showed up with ten minutes left in the class, Tawny decided to end it early.

Something big was going on, judging by the range of emotions on her friend's faces. Stacey looked slightly amused. Esther like she'd just run over Tawny's dog and didn't want to tell her. A squinty look of disbelief sat on Winnie's face, and Sasha couldn't stop smiling.

"Thanks, everyone," she said. "Great job this morning." As the customers started to move away, the Beach Clubbers closed in.

"What?" Tawny bent and pulled a towel from her bag.

She had her face covered when Stacey said, "So you and Tyler are getting married, huh?"

The towel fell, fell, fell to the ground as Tawny stared at the printout Stacey held in front of her face.

RECLUSIVE BILLIONAIRE/POKER PRINCE COMES OUT OF HIDING TO ANNOUNCE ENGAGEMENT screamed across the top of the page in big, black, bold letters.

Tawny sucked in a breath and emitted a moan as she exhaled. She ripped the paper from Stacey's grip and said, "This is bad."

"Did you think it would stay a secret?" Esther asked, slight anger coloring her tone.

"Well, no, but—" She hadn't expected it to be front page news in less than twelve hours. Tyler wasn't a celebrity—at least according to him. She also hadn't considered him a recluse, though to the rest of the world, she supposed he was.

"You guys must've really hit it off," Sasha said, pure glee on her face. "I want to hear all about it."

"It's fake," Winnie said, a little too loud.

"Shh," Tawny said at the same time Stacey did. She glanced around, but the few tourists on the beach didn't care about her love life.

"Fake or not, I want to hear about it." Sasha opened her beach chair and sat down, an expectant look in her dark honey-colored eyes.

"Now?" Tawny felt a measure of the same panic now that had infected her last night.

Stacey dropped to the sand too, one eyebrow cocked as if to say *you can't get fake engaged and then not tell. Sit and speak, sister.*

Tawny wadded up the article without reading any of the body text and settled on her mat to tell the tale.

———

By the time she finished, Tyler still hadn't texted. He'd no doubt seen the article and was doing some major damage control.

That was what she'd been reduced to: Damage control.

She sighed, sure she was going to be burnt as she hadn't put on any addition sunscreen. Sure, she spent hours in the sun, on the sand, but she always protected her skin. Her mouth was dry too, and she got up with the words, "I need a drink."

At Two Coconuts, she didn't even have to tell Mo what she wanted. Her two favorite drinks were staples on his menu, and he'd look at her and say, "Today's a cherry day," and make her fizzy cherry limeade with extra lime flavoring and double the real lime wedges. Or he'd cock his head to the side with the statement, "Feeling blue? Comin' right up." Then he'd make her blue raspberry lemon-lime concoction, with just one pump of coconut flavoring.

Today, he gave her the cherry limeade, and she wondered if that was because he knew about her recent fake engagement and how it got her heart beating faster or because her face looked like a boiled lobster from all the sun.

Didn't matter. She paid for her drink and sucked at the sugary, sweet-and-sour liquid, the burn of the carbonation down her throat the one indulgence she allowed herself every day. A couple of the other women had followed her to the beachside drink stand, and she waited in the shade while they got their refreshments.

Stacey sat beside her, nothing to drink in her hand. Of course not. Stacey preferred water above all else, and she could get that for free pretty much anywhere. "So what are you going to do?"

"I don't know." Last night, the fake engagement had seemed fine. Tyler hadn't expressed a whole lot of concern about it. She'd promised to put out her feelers and as soon as she learned Omar had left the island, they'd "break up."

The memory of how his jaw had tightened when she'd said that crawled through her mind. But she couldn't help her blunder. Couldn't go back in time and un-say it. So she'd kept her smile in place and done her best to make sure he didn't get painted with the wrong brush yet again.

And he'd been grateful she'd gone with her. As of one-thirty-three last night, he'd said thank you.

"I just need to talk to him." She took another long drink.

"Yep."

"I texted him this morning, before my class. Nothing."

"Maybe he's actually working today."

Tawny shook her head but didn't say anything. A dog barked, and she searched the beach for it. A black lab ran through the sand, skidding to a stop before picking up an object she was too far away to see.

Not Tyler. Not Lazy Bones. She'd seen them approach from the east dip in the bay, and she wondered where he lived. Probably some big mansion like Marshall's, high up in the hills, with Hank bringing him and Bones down to the beach every day to swim, surf, and waste countless hours under the sun.

"Oh." Stacey sounded surprised, and Tawny turned toward her to see her scrambling to her feet. "Tawny."

Tawny automatically stood too, though she couldn't quite see why Stacey had snapped to attention. Peering toward Sweet Breeze and then to the roadside parking lot, Tawny finally spotted the reason.

Tyler walked toward them, almost like he was in slow motion, with a wind machine blowing his hair back. It was a scene out of a movie really, at least until he arrived. Then time sped forward as she noticed he didn't smile, or touch her hand, or sweep her into one of those blissful embraces that left her jumbled for hours.

"I thought I'd find you on the beach," he finally said. He wasn't dressed for the beach, though, and his dog was nowhere in sight. Besides the tux, Tawny had never seen him in anything but board shorts and a T-shirt, so the slacks and short-sleeved blue button-up felt completely out of place, though he'd kept more buttons than necessary undone at his collar. A healthy amount of his tan chest showed through, and Tawny yanked her eyes back to his.

"I just finished a class," she said, though the workout had ended forty-five minutes ago. Thankfully, her Beach Club girls had had enough sense to scatter, leaving only Stacey and Tawny sitting together under the palm frond umbrella.

He flicked a glance at Stacey. "Can I steal her from you for a few minutes?" He was smooth, polite, casual, but Tawny sensed something teeming just beneath the surface.

"Of course, of course." Stacey practically tripped over herself to make room for Tawny to slip between her and the table where they'd been sitting. "Call me later," she hissed as Tawny passed.

With everything in her, she wanted to slip her hand into his, steal some of that seeming calmness from him, make her face as impassive as his.

She made it ten steps before she couldn't stand the silence anymore. "I'm assuming you saw the weblines this morning."

"Well, I didn't, no."

He hadn't seen them? Why hadn't he answered her text then? Why was he dressed like he'd be spending the day in an office instead of on the beach?

"But my mother called."

Tawny's heart dropped to the soles of her feet and rebounded back to its rightful place in her chest. And that hurt.

"I'm so—"

"If you say sorry one more time…." He let his words hang there as he slowed to a stop. His blue eyes stormed one moment and danced the next. She couldn't tell if he was angry, frustrated, or something else. "I don't need your apology. We just need a plan."

"A plan," she repeated, her grip tightening on her soda cup as they started walking again. "Right." The mid-day sun beat down on them, even in October, and he turned to take the walking path through the forestation along the bay.

"I told my mother we hadn't set a date yet." He strolled along, his hands in his pockets.

"Good." The truth was good. They should try to stick to that as much as possible.

"But she wants to come meet you at Christmas."

Tawny froze. "Meet me?" squeaked through her lips.

Tyler's hand found hers and latched onto it. "It's two months away," he said. "So we might have to prolong the ruse a little bit. I'm…." He stepped in front of her and gazed down at her. "We can do that, right?"

Do what? She wasn't sure because of how he watched

her with those ocean-blue eyes. She nodded, trying to get her thoughts to make sense.

"Great." He gave her an easy smile. "So I think you're right. We need to get some facts in line. I'll get you a diamond ring. And we'll make sure that everything is in place for when my family comes for the holidays."

Get some facts in line.

Make sure everything is in place for when my family comes for the holidays.

So he didn't genuinely like her. The old Tawny would've been secretly plotting how she could get him to fall madly in love with her. But the Tawny walking down the breezeway with Tyler's hand in hers needed to ask a few questions. She tugged him over to a driftwood bench, where they sat down. "Okay, so let me just get a few things straight."

"Straight is good."

"Yeah, so…you're okay continuing the ruse, because…."

He chuckled and ducked his head, that delicious beard calling to her. Why couldn't he have shaved? Did he know she had a weakness for scruffy surfers?

He glanced up, right into her eyes. "You really want to know?"

"I find the truth refreshing, don't you?" She tried to smile, but an earthquake was happening with her internal organs. She doubted she'd even be able to hear anything he said.

"I may have told my mom that yes, we were in a good place and would definitely still be together at Christmas."

He looked sheepish and he ducked his head in true bashful form. "But if you don't want to play along that long, I get it. We can do a few weeks, like we planned, and then I'll call her and say it's over."

Tawny didn't like the sound of over, but she couldn't say that. Of course Tyler would want this ruse to end as quickly as possible, but he was the one who'd told his mother to come for Christmas. Nothing made sense, so she shelved the confusing words to dwell on later.

"Why are we holding hands right now?" she asked.

"There's a couple of reporters following me around." He glanced down the path, and Tawny followed his gaze but couldn't see anyone.

"And I'm going to wear a fake diamond."

"Well, it'll be a real diamond, but the engagement is still fake." He searched her face. "Right?"

"Of course." She couldn't get engaged to the guy a week after talking to him—*really* talking to him—for the first time. She wasn't going to slip and tell him she'd been watching him for months. He didn't need to know that.

"What else did you tell your mom?"

"Just that I'd met a sweet girl and things had happened fast, and I'd tell her more about it when I wasn't so tired." He looked across the breezeway and toward the bay. "Then I got her talking about the gala, and she didn't come back to the engagement."

"So all true things."

"Well, you are sweet." He gave her a lopsided grin that made her heart flip. "And things did happen fast. So." He shrugged. "I wasn't technically lying, which is a good thing, because my New Yorker mother can smell a lie from thousands of miles away—through phone lines." He laughed, the joy in his voice and on his face testifying of his love for his mother.

Tawny sobered. Her own mother would've flipped out about an engagement, any engagement, and she was suddenly glad her mom wasn't here so she wouldn't have to lie to her. Or get her hopes up.

"So, how about dinner tonight to get some facts straight?" He stood and headed back toward Two Coconuts. "I have a couple of things to do, but I can meet as early as four."

"Four o'clock for dinner? What are we? Sixty-five?"

This time when he laughed, he could've painted the entire sky with happiness. He pulled her close and said, "First fact, I like to joke and laugh. So keep that coming."

She stepped into his arms, enjoying the easy way his hands slid along her waist, and the feel of his beard beneath her fingertips. He let her explore the planes of his face, and the moment between them went quickly from fake to real—at least for her.

"How about a kiss for the camera?"

She startled toward the male voice to find three of them standing there, two pointing cameras in her direction and one holding out a recording device.

"No comment," Tyler said, his voice completely different than the husky murmur with which he'd just spoken. "And no pictures, guys. You got enough at the gala last night."

"Where's your ring?" one of them asked anyway.

"Getting sized," Tawny said, a repeat from one of the interviews from the previous night.

Tyler glared and brought Tawny past the reporters.

"Really? No kiss from the Poker Prince?"

Tyler whipped back to the man so fast, Tawny's pulse increased and her adrenaline spiked. For one terrible moment, she thought he'd clock the man right in the mouth. "Don't. Call me that," he growled instead.

The Poker Prince. She'd have to look up what that meant later. Or simply ask Tyler, but she wasn't going to do it in front of reporters. It felt like an intimate piece of his past that his fiancée should know.

"Plenty of pictures of you kissing women on the Internet," the man said, utterly nonplussed. "Just give us one of you and your fiancée."

"Not today." Tyler turned around and strode faster now. Tawny did her best to keep up, wondering how he could go from hot to cold so dang fast. And who all those other women were. A green seed of jealousy planted itself inside her heart, though it was ridiculous to think he'd never been in a relationship before.

This isn't a real relationship, she thought.

"One kiss?" the guy called after them, and the thought of kissing Tyler had Tawny's heart bouncing in anticipation.

"We could just give them—" she started, but he glared her into silence. She saw a little bit of what he probably used to win poker hands in that ice-cold stare, and she almost shivered.

"I'm not kissing you for the first time for a camera." He

pressed his lips into a tight line, shook his head, and said, "I'll call you later to arrange dinner."

She'd lost the ability to move, apparently, because all she could do was stare after him.

Kissing you for the first time....

So there'd be a first kiss. And he wanted it to be private. Right?

So much for no strings attached.

She turned away from his retreating form, but she didn't want to give another interview. She blinked at the reporters standing there and went back to get her bag which she'd left with Stacey at Two Coconuts, wishing she didn't feel quite so tied to Tyler already.

SEVEN

TYLER MADE it to the safety of his car without encountering anyone else. Thankfully. His whole head buzzed, and not in a good way. Or maybe in a good way. He wasn't sure. He rubbed his fingers along his forehead, trying to get his brain to shut off.

But ever since his mother had called that morning, his thoughts had been streaming, circling, swirling in his head.

Tawny acted like she liked him, but that had to be because of his willingness to go along with her fake relationship. "Just until Omar leaves town," he told himself for at least the twentieth time that day.

He pulled onto the road, nowhere really to be for another hour, but he'd spent plenty of time driving the winding roads around the island. Sometimes the scent of the wind and the sound of the surf helped him work out problems.

Prolonging their relationship was a big problem. So was establishing some facts between them. He didn't want to tell her about his life in LA, Las Vegas, or New York City. He didn't want her to see the pictures of him with various women. And he certainly didn't want her to know his poker nickname or how quickly he'd risen to fame.

The youngest professional poker player to make a million dollars....

The best up and coming poker player in the world....

The Poker Prince does it again! Another win, another million, another all-nighter....

Tyler had the headlines memorized, unfortunately. He'd stopped reading the headlines and getting on the Internet after his second big win, but sometimes he heard things, saw something on a billboard, or someone had the TV on in the background.

Short of moving to the middle of nowhere and shutting down the WiFi, it was pretty hard to get completely away from everything.

He pulled over and parked before getting out and walking down the public beach on the opposite side of the bay from where Fisher's hotel stood and where Tawny taught her yoga classes. He could hope the reporters would find another story, and he tossed a prayer heavenward that something big would happen and his fake engagement would fade into oblivion.

He'd learned how to stay off the radar, and that included keeping himself to a small radius of space. His beach house. His private beach. His dog. A few restaurants. No one cared what he was doing with his billions in Hawaii until something like this happened.

He pushed his breath out, thinking about Tawny in her stringy T-shirts and bright pink sports bras. She was cute, and he couldn't believe he'd waited for this hospital gala to ask her out. What would've happened if she hadn't made up the engagement?

Would he have asked her out again?

Tyler honestly didn't know. He'd told her no strings attached, it wasn't a date, and so many other things just to get her to say yes.

"And you have to stick to that," he told himself. She'd gone along with his hand-holding, his strange embraces, but probably because she was grateful for the dress or simply awe-struck with his money.

After all, historically, women didn't show interest in him *before* they knew about his bank account. So why would Tawny?

She wouldn't.

Tyler got through the video conferencing with his accountants in LA, something he forced himself to do once a month. His guys were great, and allowed him to call in on Sunday afternoon. He dressed up and they dressed down, and they talked for a couple of hours about what Tyler's money was doing, and what it could be doing, and what it should be doing.

He didn't hate that he had the money, and he didn't

want to squander it. He just didn't want to talk about a four-year period of his life he'd rather forget. He wasn't sure Tawny needed to know every detail of his life on the professional poker circuit, and he decided he'd give her surface stuff.

He changed out of his button-up shirt and slacks and put on his board shorts. The hammock called to him, as he'd been out late the night before and gotten up way too early to the sound of his mother's angry voice.

After shoving his phone in his pocket, he relaxed in the hammock and closed his eyes. He couldn't fall asleep though, despite his fatigue. Tawny dominated his thoughts, and he hated that they had to meet to get some facts about each other.

It sounded so clinical and nothing like what he wanted to spend his time doing. But with the bloodhound reporters still hanging around, if he didn't spend a free evening with his supposed fiancée, their suspicions would be raised.

His phone buzzed, but he ignored it. His brother had called during his meeting too, and Tyler had texted to say he'd call him later.

Apparently, it was later.

Tyler didn't care. He only had a few more hours before he had to go meet a beautiful woman and pretend not to like her. Or was he pretending to be in love with her?

Tyler wasn't sure, and that drove him toward the edge of madness.

When he woke, he wasn't sure where he was or what time is was. The sky held hues of navy and gold, and the wind brushed against his loose hair. He'd cut it himself on Saturday morning, a skill he'd acquired while on the poker circuit so he could clean up whenever he wanted.

He took a moment to enjoy the serenity of the scene before him. The sky, the water, the golden sand. It was everything he'd wanted when he'd come to the island, and he held onto the peace of it for as long as possible.

Then he pulled out his phone and forced himself to check his many messages. A sigh passed through his whole body, driving frustration into his bloodstream. A tiny 32 sat on his messaging app, which meant Wayne had decided to text out his lecture instead of waiting for Tyler to return his calls.

He'd also missed six phone calls. He wasn't even sure six people had his phone number, so he started there.

Three calls from Wayne, two from Tawny, and one from Jasper.

Tyler decided to go with the easiest of the three, and that was Jasper. "You called?" He continued to swing in the hammock, as it was only five-thirty and surely still too early for dinner with Tawny.

"Yeah, you said you'd send me the contact info for your mutual fund guy."

"Oh, right." Tyler had said that, and he was actually glad this conversation had nothing to do with his personal life. "I'll text it right now."

"Thanks. I think I'm ready to do something a little more aggressive with my investments."

"Who are you using?"

"Infinity Investments?" The fact that Jasper phrased it

as a question meant he hadn't done all the homework on the company. At least not what Tyler would've done.

"You should talk to Lexie. Her firm is top-notch."

"Are you with her?"

"Her company," Tyler said. "My accountants and investment bankers are out of LA. I'll send you what I've got."

"Great, thanks." The call ended, and Tyler appreciated the quick, business-like way he could interact with his billionaire friends. After all, they were all busy. Well, Tyler wasn't, but everyone else seemed to have a never-ending to-do list.

He chose to listen to his voicemail messages next and found that Tawny hadn't left any. He put off calling her back because he teetered on the edge of indecision. Maybe he shouldn't go to dinner with her. Maybe they should just do the one-time thing and move on. Who cared what the papers said? Or what the major weblines said?

Something else would come up, and everyone would forget about him like they had before. And he could waste a few more months of his life and then ask Tawny out for real. Tons of strings attached.

He didn't want to talk to his brother either, so he stayed in the hammock doing nothing. A dog barked, alerting him to the fact that he had no idea where Lazy Bones was. Not that it mattered. The golden retriever never wandered far, and he was probably lying in the shade nearby, his favorite patch near the trio of pineapple plants Tyler cultivated himself. Marshall had given him the suckers to plant, and he'd actually been pleased and surprised to watch the foliage grow and produce something he could eat.

Lazy Bones wasn't there, and another bark sounded, this one closer. Tyler stood and walked to the edge of the trees so he could look both ways down the beach.

He found his dog trotting along, certainly not in any hurry.

Right behind him was a certain brown-haired woman who'd turned Tyler's life upside down in a matter of seconds.

He became acutely aware that he wasn't wearing a shirt as Tawny drew closer. "Your dog found me," she said. "I swear I didn't come searching for your place." She arrived in front of him and peered behind him to the hammock, the back yard that was littered with dog toys and Frisbees, his surfboards, wetsuits, boogie boards, and flippers.

Tyler didn't turn. He knew what his yard looked like. "We're sort of neighbors."

"Yeah." She looked back the way she'd come. "I only live about a half a mile from here. Different neighborhood though."

He nodded, as he'd been to her house before.

"I can't believe this is where you live." She stepped past him, and he twisted to watch her. She touched the rope of his hammock and scanned the simple house. He'd painted it blue a couple of years ago, and it could stand a new coat, in all honesty.

"This is where I live."

She locked eyes with him. "How many bedrooms is this?"

"Just the one." Always one. Tyler had gotten very good at living for one. It wasn't until he'd asked Tawny out that he'd even considered a life built for two.

"Really?"

"Why are you so surprised?" Tyler didn't think he spoke too harshly, but Tawny's eyes rounded as if he had.

She shrugged and backed up a few steps. "Private beach?"

"Yes. Same as you."

Her hair brushed her shoulders as she cocked her head. Tyler fisted his fingers to keep from touching her. After all, there was no one watching now, and he didn't want to dangle his heart from a limb, only to watch it fall and break.

"You're a billionaire," she said as if he didn't know. "I can afford this place, and trust me, I'm not a billionaire." She spoke in a half-coy voice, but she didn't laugh and didn't smile.

"So maybe the first fact you should know about me," he said. "Is that I don't care about my money."

She scoffed as if he'd just said the stupidest thing on the planet. "Everyone cares about money, Tyler." His name rolled off her tongue easily, and he wanted to hear her say it again and then again, preferably right before he kissed her.

"Yeah, okay." He bent down and scrubbed Lazy Bones, who looked up at him with eagerness in his eyes, like *didn't I do great, Dad? Didn't I? I brought Tawny to you. I did great.*

"I care about money," he said. "I guess I just don't care about throwing it around."

Her eyes sparkled as she watched him for a moment past comfortable. "Interesting," she finally said. "So I called you a couple of times. You didn't answer."

He pointed to the hammock. "Napping. Another fact about me. I lay here every afternoon and listen to the waves as they come into the bay."

She turned back to the pristine water, which looked almost black in the fading light. Twilight was Tyler's favorite time of day. The sunset reminded him that he was still human, still living under the same sky he always had, still breathing through another day.

"What do they say?" she asked.

"Who?"

"Not who." She pointed to the waves. "What. The waves."

"They don't say anything." He stepped beside her, maybe an inch or two too close.

She glanced up at him. "Then you're not listening very well."

So she was one of those existential people. He should've known, what with the yoga and all. She sat in his hammock, and he wasn't sure how he felt about it. He'd only had a handful of people over to his house— Fisher, Marshall, Jasper, the other Hawaii Nine-0 members. They'd stuck to the house, and sharing his hammock with Tawny felt as right as it did wrong.

"Did you want to go to dinner?" she finally asked.

"Yeah, we better." He exhaled as he turned back to the house. "Let me grab a shirt." As he went, he reminded himself that this was not a date. He could *not* hold her hand just because he wanted to. Any physical contact had to be because there were people watching. People that needed to be convinced that he and Tawny were engaged. People who could pass the message on to Omar, who would then leave the island thinking Tawny was on her way to wedded bliss.

Even if that couldn't be further from the truth. He pulled a light blue T-shirt over his head and quickly wet his hair and pushed it out of his face. "You can do this," he told his reflection. For Tawny and her safety. To protect her. He could pretend, for her.

Too bad it wasn't all that hard to act like he liked her, and the time spent with her was no problem for Tyler at all.

EIGHT

TAWNY WISHED he'd chosen a more public place. Well, the sushi house was public, but it wasn't busy. And with only a handful of people in the restaurant—none of whom seemed to care that Tawny and Tyler were there— there was no reason to hold his hand. No reason to cuddle into him. No reason to lean forward and laugh like he'd just told the funniest joke on the planet.

She knew tons of little tidbits about him and his life now, but for some reason, she didn't care. So he liked jokes. He took a nap every day. He had a photographic memory—that had been a good source of conversation for half the meal.

But what she wanted to know—what drove him? Why did he quit playing poker? Sell his company? Why had he chosen Getaway Bay as his new home? How did he think? —she couldn't ask. At least if she wanted to keep pretending that the feelings rippling through her were fake.

She'd refused to allow herself to look anything up on the Internet. She knew better than most that *any*one could put *any*thing on the Internet like it was true. So she ate her crab rangoons and as many spicy tuna rolls as she could stomach, wishing this date felt real at all.

The other times she'd been out with Tyler had been easy, casual. This felt like work, and she didn't like it.

"Should we go?" he asked, tossing his napkin on the table.

"Sure. I'm stuffed." And maybe there would be a reporter or two lurking outside the restaurant.

He paid and they went out into the beautiful evening. "What are you doing for the holidays?" he asked, his hands tucked safely in his pockets.

She swung her purse, trying to flirt a little with him. "Oh, probably just going over to Aloha Hideaway for the Thanksgiving feast."

"You don't go visit anyone?"

She thought about the father she hadn't seen in two decades. "I sometimes go to Arizona to see my brother," she said. "But not this year. He's taking his family on a cruise for Christmas, and I've spent more than my fair share on a ship like that."

Tyler glanced at her, curiosity on his face. "Oh yeah?"

"Yeah, before I worked in Cancun—and met Omar." She waved her hand, realizing she finally had something to thank the man for—forcing her and Tyler together after the gala. "I worked on cruise ships from here to Puerto Rico, Grand Cayman, even did an Alaskan line."

"And you didn't like them." He wasn't asking, and she was learning that he was extremely perceptive, which she supposed fit with his poker success.

"They were okay," she said. "Some good tippers. But not everyone eats free on the ship." She lifted one shoulder in a shrug. "I did it for about six years, so it wasn't horrible."

"Did what?"

"Taught water aerobics on one ship. Poolside yoga on another. On one line, I had to fill in as the masseuse, even though I'm not a licensed massage therapist." The memories of her time on the ships wasn't completely unhappy. "It is lonely work though," she murmured, realizing too late that she'd said it out loud.

"Playing poker is a bit like that," he said, his voice as equally as soft. "Lonely."

She wanted to hold his hand so badly, and it took everything in her to just keep swinging her purse. "I imagine so. It's always lonely at the top."

He let several steps go by in silence. "Did you look me up?" he asked.

"No," she said, maybe a little too quickly.

He cocked one eyebrow in challenge.

"I didn't," she insisted. "Like I want to see you sucking face with other women." The very thought left her cold, though surely a man like Tyler hadn't had to beg for female attention. He still didn't. He chose his life of isolation, in a tiny one-bedroom beach house, with a golden retriever for a friend.

A sense of inadequacy descended on Tawny. He'd met her months ago, and it was clear he wasn't interested. She clenched her arms across her chest, wishing she could just turn her mind off. Just for a moment.

They turned a corner, and Tawny paused. A man had just come out of the shop up ahead, and he looked dangerously like Omar. "Hold my hand," she hissed.

"What?" Tyler followed her gaze and withdrew his hand from his pocket at the same time Omar turned toward them, a cigar pressed between his lips. He lifted his hands to light it, his eyes never leaving Tawny.

She threw her head back and laughed as she grabbed onto Tyler's arm with both of her hands. She leaned into him and sort of dragged him along as they continued toward Omar. She pretended not to see him until the very last moment, and then she startled. "Oh. Hello, Omar."

He grunted and sized up Tyler, apparently finding him a bit too tall, or too muscular. Something, because Omar didn't normally back down from a fight.

"Still here?" Tyler asked, his arm tightening against his side, keeping Tawny right next to him.

"That's right, hombre."

"What do you do on the island again?" Tyler asked.

"None of your—"

"Avocados," Tawny said. "How long will you be here, Omar?"

He glared at Tyler for another moment. "I don't know. Could be a while."

Tawny sighed like his presence on the island was frustrating—because it was. But another part of her was secretly glad that she and Tyler would need to continue their charade until he left.

"I'm surprised you can leave your empire in Mexico," Tyler said.

"You left yours in New York City." Omar seemed to sense that he'd won, because he smirked and walked away, his ridiculous white shoes a slap in the face to life on a Hawaiian island.

Tawny waited until he turned the corner, and then she carefully slipped her hand out of Tyler's. "He's...I can't believe I ever dated him."

Tyler turned back the way they'd been going, and they passed the cigar shop Omar had come out of. "Why did you?"

"Date him? Oh, I suppose I thought he was handsome, and he threw his money around, and brought me drinks at work. That kind of stuff."

Tyler nodded. "So you like it when a man dotes on you."

"It doesn't hurt. And you forgot the handsome part." She tried to play off the conversation as nothing while she searched for why she had dated Omar.

"I brought you a drink at work."

"And you're handsome." At least this flirting was real.

He paused at the next corner and gazed down at her. Something resided in his eyes that she couldn't identify. But it was intense and strong and when he opened his mouth, she almost expected him to blurt out that he wished their relationship was real.

Instead, he said, "We should head back."

———

The next morning, three men attended Tawny's beachside yoga class. It was obvious none of them had so much as bent over to touch their toes in a while, and not just from the stark farmer's tan on the one guy's biceps.

All three of them lingered after the class, like they had some deep, burning question about connecting to Mother Earth or how they could increase their flexibility.

She knew who they were, and she lifted her hand and said, "No comment, guys," before any of them could speak.

"Come on," the dark-haired one said, frustration in both words. "Give us something."

"What do you want to know?" Tawny shouldered her bag. If they wanted to talk, they'd have to walk with her, because the sun shone hot that day.

"Have you set a date?" a blond man asked, tapping on his phone like crazy.

"Nope."

"Why don't you wear a diamond ring?"

"It's getting sized," she said in a monotone. She'd answered that one before.

"Why hasn't anyone on the island seen you two together before the gala?"

Tawny stumbled in the sand and almost went down.

"How should I know?" she asked, her voice acidic. "It's not like we took selfies and flashed them for the world to see."

"But even the regulars," he pressed, a little weasel-faced man with hair the color of dirt. "Mo at Two Coconuts, the valet at Sweet Breeze, where both you and Tyler visit quite often. They were all as surprised by the engagement as we were."

Tawny's heart froze for a moment and when it burst out of the ice it had been encased in, it pumped three times as fast. He'd spoken to Sterling? What had the valet said about her? An internal groan almost touched her vocal chords.

"I gotta go, guys. It was fun chatting. Please don't bother me at work again." She skipped Two Coconuts, though she had been planning to stop for a drink. Mo. She shook her head. What had he said?

Probably nothing, she told herself as she put her duffle bag over her shoulders like a backpack and bent to unlock her bicycle. He had a business to run; he didn't have time to gossip about nothing.

Which was exactly what Tyler and Tawny had had before the gala. Nothing. And how long would it be before those three reporters figured that out?

When she got home, she dialed Tyler's number, wondering if he'd be in from surfing yet. He'd told her he liked to go out first thing in the morning and surf until the waves died. She had no idea when that happened, and if there was one thing she knew about Tyler, it was that he didn't keep to a schedule.

Sure enough, the call went to voicemail, and she said, "I think we have a problem. Call me back when you get this." She let her bag fall to the floor. "Oh, and I need a diamond ring ASAP. Maybe we could go this afternoon?"

She nodded to herself and hung up, hoping the waves died really, really soon.

NINE

TYLER LET the waves wash him in and out, in and out, like breathing. He loved being in the ocean, loved the kiss of sunshine on his skin, loved listening to the waves. And today, he was actually trying to hear what they were saying.

He couldn't quite make out any words, but by the time he finally stood and took his surfboard back to shore, every muscle in his body had calmed. He showered, fed Bones, and picked up his phone.

Tawny had called, and her message erased all the peace he'd managed to find in the ocean that morning. He didn't have much on his schedule, honestly, so a plan started to form in his mind.

They'd been telling everyone that her ring was getting sized, and he didn't want to go into any jeweler and try to explain the situation now.

So he called Jasper, who worked in the diamond industry and could hopefully get Tyler a private meeting with someone on the island. Someone who could be discreet.

"It's a bit early, don't you think?" Jasper yawned, and it sounded like he wasn't too happy Tyler had called.

"Early?" Tyler glanced around but he didn't own a clock. "I have no idea what time it is."

"Well, I work in the middle of the night. Belgium is on a twelve-hour time difference."

Guilt sliced through Tyler. "Sorry. Um, I just have a quick favor. Can you meet me at your shop? I need...." Wow, he couldn't even say it. "I need—" He exhaled and told himself to just say it. "So you've probably heard I'm engaged, and I need a ring pretty much yesterday, and I need to be able to go into the front of the shop and act like I'm picking it up after waiting for it to get sized."

It sounded so stupid coming out of his mouth. To Jasper's credit, he just gave one long hiss as he blew out his breath. "You got engaged?"

"It's...fake." He could trust Jasper.

"Fake? Tyler, come on."

"It's a long story, and you were up all night with Belgium."

Jasper laughed. "Fine. I know how you like your privacy."

Tyler did like his privacy. It was why he'd flown six hours west of where he'd grown up, where he'd made his money, where his family lived. His jaw tightened. "I just— can you help me with the ring?"

"I'm sure I can."

"Today?"

"Can I sleep for a few hours?"

"Sure, how about later this afternoon? Four or five?"

Jasper yawned and confirmed for later that day, and Tyler hung up. He should probably tell the other members of the Nine-0 club about the fake engagement, but he liked to lay low during meetings. They were business meetings, not personal problem meetings. Still, he was a bit surprised neither Marshall nor Fisher had called yet.

But they probably didn't pay attention to the gossip headlines the way some people did. Tyler himself wouldn't have seen anything on the Internet if not for his mother.

He dialed Tawny next, his heart doing a little hop, skip, and jump when she answered in that sweet voice of hers.

"So I've spoken to a friend, and we can go pick up your ring this afternoon."

"Is that so?" The fun, flirty tone of her voice was a welcome addition to Tyler's life, and a pang of regret lanced through him when he reminded himself he wouldn't be able to keep her forever. Or even past Christmas.

"That is so," he said. "Maybe we could grab some lunch and take our afternoon siesta together. We can't go to the jeweler until later, around five tonight."

"Oh, a man after my own heart." She giggled, the sound worming its way straight into Tyler's heart. "An afternoon siesta sounds amazing."

Tyler agreed but as he did, he worried about sharing

his hammock and his beach with Tawny. It was simply a foreign concept for him to allow someone too far into his life. At the same time, it felt good to have her only a phone call away.

"You realize it's almost lunch time right now," she said. "Don't you?"

Tyler didn't want to admit he hadn't known that. "Yeah, um, yeah. Where do you want to meet?"

"You so did not know it was lunchtime." She laughed, and he wished they were in the same space so he could hear her voice as it lifted into the sky.

He chuckled too. "Fine. I don't know what time it is."

"It's almost noon," she said. "And I'm feeling like American fare today."

"Because you ate a dozen tuna rolls yesterday."

"A dozen? Come on." She obviously wore a smile because it carried in her tone. "The Breezeway? Twenty minutes?"

Tyler enjoyed the restaurant on the first floor of Fisher's hotel. "Sure," he said. "See you there."

He arrived at The Breezeway nineteen minutes later to find her perched on a barstool, a glass of clear liquid in front of her. She wore a flowing pale pink cover-up with bright yellow straps going over her shoulders. Beach wear.

Tyler smiled as she tucked her hair behind her ear and glanced around. Watching her like this, he could see the vulnerability on her face that she normally kept masked. He could admire her beauty without her being able to see it, without having to hide it.

He became aware of someone standing next to him, and he cut a look out of the corner of his eye to see the same dark-haired reporter who'd been hanging around the island.

"Don't you have something better to do?" Tyler couldn't help the bite in his voice. "I'm not even anyone special."

"Do you know the percentage of the population who are billionaires?" He gave Tyler a look that wasn't malicious. "It's like one out of every four million. Whatever this is." He gestured between Tyler and Tawny. "It's something."

Not for the first time, Tyler cursed his money. And he kept his mouth shut about the eight other people—and potentially three more—people who had nine zeroes in their bank accounts who lived right here on the island.

"This is nothing," Tyler said, wishing he wasn't speaking quite so true. "Now, if you'll excuse me, I'm going to eat lunch with my fiancée." He paused and turned back, taking in the man's features. Brown eyes. Dark hair. Tan. Perfectly symmetrical face. He had the perfect face for those tiny pictures next to by-lines.

"Can I ask you something?" he asked.

"Sure," the guy said.

"What if I needed some information on someone? An owner of a couple of avocado farms here on the island."

A light entered the man's dark eyes. "Well, you might hire someone."

"How much for you to find out everything you can

about someone for me?" Tyler glanced over his shoulder to see if Tawny had spotted him yet. She drank from her glass, still unaware of his presence. She probably thought he was late, maybe thinking he wouldn't come at all.

"Depends on who it is."

"Okay, well, how about you give me your name and number, and we can talk about it."

The man narrowed his eyes, and Tyler simply stared back, easily slipping into his poker face. He reached into his pocket and pulled out a card. "Jason Barnes, from Aces High."

Tyler's heart catapulted around his chest, but he took the card without so much as blinking. "The poker magazine? Why are you here?"

"There're a lot of people who'd love to see you come back to the pro circuit."

"Never gonna happen."

"No?" Jason's eyebrows lifted. "Don't you miss it?"

"Not even a little bit." He waved the card. "Thanks." He walked away, shoving the card in his pocket so Tawny wouldn't know he was considering hiring a reporter to find the dirt on Omar Velasquez.

"Hey." He bent down and pressed his lips to her cheek. "Sorry I'm late." One arm slipped effortlessly around her waist as he added, "Don't look, but there's a reporter watching."

She giggled, her acting absolutely flawless. One hand came up and touched his face, sending sparks through his jaw and down the right side of his neck.

Their eyes locked, and Tyler felt a measure of craziness

move through him. Because he found himself leaning closer, his eyes drifting closed in tandem with hers. His mouth touched hers a moment later, and a moan slipped up his throat.

Tawny's other hand came up and curled around the back of his neck, holding him close as the kiss dragged on, deepened, drew him toward the edge of madness.

She seemed utterly in control of herself, but Tyler's every nerve went wild. When she finally had the wherewithal to pull away, she kept her face close to his, and he was pleased that her breathing was as ragged as his.

What that meant, he didn't know. What he did know was that this was no longer an act for him. He wanted to kiss her like that every morning, every evening, and every minute in between.

"What were you drinking?" he whispered.

"Just water." She leaned back, breaking the bubble that had formed around them. Tyler couldn't help it; he glanced toward where Jason had been standing. He remained there, his phone out and pointed in Tyler's direction.

When he caught Tyler looking, he raised his hand in acknowledgement, turned, and walked away.

"Is he gone?" Tawny asked, her body still leaning into his.

Tyler sighed as he sat on the stool next to her. "Yeah." He touched his lips, which felt a bit slick from her lip gloss. A smile stole across his face, and thankfully, a waitress appeared and asked if they'd like a table.

"Yes," he said with relief. "Yes, we'd like a table." Then

he could hide behind a menu while he relived the best kiss of his life.

———

A skin of tension hovered over him during lunch. Finally, he said, "I hope that wasn't too awkward."

She hadn't said a whole lot of anything, and that was unusual for her. She was flirty, and chatty, and usually had this vibrant energy about her.

"The kiss?"

"Yeah." Tyler looked her right in the eyes, trying to figure out if he was the only one feeling like this relationship could be real if one of them would just admit it. He wasn't going to though, because he couldn't decipher anything in her gaze.

"It was fine."

"Ouch." Tyler chuckled. "I mean, it's been a while for me, but I was hoping it would be better than fine."

A blush crawled into her cheeks, and Tyler finally got the first hint that his kiss was more than fine. But was it welcome?

"It's been a while for you?"

"Almost a decade," he admitted.

Her eyes rounded. "Since you kissed someone?"

"Since any relationship," he said. "Even a fake one."

She blinked, her mouth hanging open slightly. After a moment she seemed to recover and she pulled her fruity soda closer and took a long drink. "I find that hard to believe."

He shrugged. "It's the truth."

"Why? Did something happen? You don't want to get married?" Did he imagine the interest in her voice? The earnestness in her face?

Tyler had not told anyone why he didn't date. He hadn't had to, because people left him alone in Hawaii. And for the few years before he sold his half of PokerPlay-Now.com, he'd been so busy getting the world's first online poker website up and running, he hadn't had time for women.

Plus, there was Holly....

"I'd marry the right person," he said carefully, trying to find his way through this landmine of conversation.

"But you don't date."

"I didn't, no."

Tawny cocked her head, as if trying to hear more behind the words. Tyler lifted his own soda to his lips, realizing he'd just implied that he didn't date before he met her. Before them, like maybe they were dating.

"I...." He set his glass down and schooled his emotions behind his poker face. "My last girlfriend wasn't really a girlfriend." Embarrassed heat filled him. "More like a one-night stand who got pregnant."

Tawny sucked in a breath and said, "Oh."

Tyler leaned onto his forearms and tried to convey to her that this was serious, this was real. "I haven't told anyone this. Not even Jasper, or Fisher. I would appreciate it if you didn't tell anyone."

"Of course I won't."

"Even after we 'break up'." He used air quotes around the last two words.

"Why did you tell me at all?"

Why had he? Tyler sighed and leaned back in the booth. "I wanted you to know," he said simply. And he did want her to know. It felt like something he'd have to tell someone he was getting serious with—and they were supposed to be engaged.

Or did he just feel like things between them were ten times more serious now that he'd kissed her?

"So, did you get married? You've got a kid in New York or something?" Tawny fiddled with her discarded straw wrapper.

Tyler shook his head, the memories, the lights, the glitz, the glam streaming through his head though he studied the tabletop. "No."

"No?"

He glanced up. "I tried to do the right thing. I said I'd marry her and all that. We weren't quite to the announcement phase yet, and she didn't have a ring, before she lost the pregnancy." And he'd never been so relieved. He and Holly weren't a match, and he'd known it the night he'd met her.

But she was exotic, and beautiful, and he'd been high off another world championship win. That, combined with too much alcohol...had led him here to Getaway Bay.

"I quit the pro circuit after that championship," he said as if he'd filled in all the details he kept in his head. "Started the online game site with my brother Wayne." He exhaled and waited while the waitress arrived with their food. "Haven't dated since."

She picked up her crispy chicken sandwich and paused before taking a bite. "Do you miss poker?"

"No."

"Not even a little?"

"Not even a little."

"You won a lot, didn't you?"

"I did." It was refreshing to give the details he wanted to give about his past, and a rush of affection for Tawny had his face heating again. "I was the fastest-rising poker player in the world. I made the most too, for about three years. Then Holly happened, and I quit, and Wayne and I focused on the website."

She wiped her lips and swallowed. "Were you a billionaire before the website?"

"Not quite." He started eating his burger, glad the atmosphere between them had relaxed. "So enough about me. What about you?"

"What about me?"

"Past relationships? Seems like something your fiancé would know."

"Yes, it does." But she continued eating. When she finished her sandwich, she began pushing around her fruit. "So you know about Omar."

"A little," Tyler hedged, the card in his pocket suddenly burning against his skin.

"Since coming to the island, I've dated a few men. Nobody special."

"No? Why not?"

"Unlucky in love." She pointed to herself. "My last name fits me so well."

Tyler had no idea when the words entered his mind, or why he let them out of his mouth. But when he said, "Maybe that's about to change," he was as shocked as Tawny looked.

TEN

MAYBE THAT'S ABOUT *to change.*

Tawny couldn't get the words out of her head. What had he meant by that? The way he held her hand as they walked into the jewelry store felt real. And that kiss.... Fireworks popped through her bloodstream just thinking about it. She really hoped she'd get to experience another kiss from him, because she hadn't quite been prepared for the first one.

A tall, sandy-haired man stood behind the counter, wearing an expensive suit and a smile. "Tyler."

"Jasper." Tyler and Jasper did quick patting of backs, and Tyler stepped back. "This is my fiancée, Tawny Loveless. Tawny, this is a good friend of mine, Jasper Rosequist."

"Nice to meet you." She cut a glance at Tyler as she stepped forward and shook Jasper's hand. "Doesn't he know?" she whispered out of the corner of her mouth.

Tyler brought her close, his hand along her waist like fire, and leaned down as if they were going to share an intimate secret. "He does, yes. But you never know who's watching or listening."

Of course. She reminded herself that he was continuing this ruse for her, because he was a nice guy. Not because he liked her. Not because the heated passion in that kiss had been real.

"I've got your ring right here." Jasper brought out a velvet tray which held a diamond ring that Tawny couldn't help gawking at.

"This is it?"

"It's okay?" Tyler searched her face, and Tawny didn't hate the way he probed with his eyes to find information. But what she was really feeling—*I wish this wasn't a fake diamond ring*—she kept carefully masked. She had to. This was his *life*. He was a celebrity, no matter how much he tried to tell her he wasn't. The three reporters who'd joined her class that morning were proof of that.

She would not lose her heart to a lie. "Yes, it's fine." She swallowed and held out her left hand so Jasper could slip the ring on. It was more than fine, and she felt like it would weigh down her whole arm. But it didn't, and she tilted her hand to admire the glittering gem. She grinned as she looked at Tyler. "It's perfect. Thank you."

It felt like a moment she'd tip up on her toes, wrap her arms around his neck, and kiss him. Her body flinched toward his, but she stopped herself from making a fool of herself.

Tyler knocked twice on the glass case, and said, "Thanks, Jasper."

"Anytime." The man looked back and forth between Tyler and Tawny, his eyes alight and his smile wide. "And just so you know, the same two guys have walked by three times. So be on your game when you go."

Tawny's stomach twisted, but Tyler took her hand in his, calming her, comforting her. He seemed strong and in control as they moved toward the door and pushed out into the Hawaiian heat.

"So you like it?" he asked, maybe a bit too loud.

Tawny squealed, most of the enthusiasm in the sound absolutely real. "I love it." She did throw herself into his arms now, glad when he laughed and drew her right against his chest. "Thank you," she said again, unsure of why she felt the need to keep expressing her gratitude to him.

He bent down and she lifted up, and this second kiss felt like magic in her veins. He certainly knew how to kiss a woman like he felt something for her, and she couldn't believe he hadn't dated anyone in almost a decade.

You're not dating him either, she told herself. But the words were very easy to silence with Tyler's lips moving so deliciously against hers.

She didn't want the kiss to end, but he eventually pulled back, flushed and breathless, the same as her. He tucked her into his side and they walked toward the two men staring open-mouthed at them. As they passed, Tawny lifted her left hand to show them her diamond, a giggle trickling from her throat.

And honestly, she was happier than she'd been in a long, long time. She just hoped that when this ended in a couple of months, she hadn't given him her heart.

———

The engagement ring shone in the light from her phone as both rested on her nightstand. She lay in bed, feeling like a fraud. Omar hadn't even tried to contact her. She hadn't seen any of his goons hanging around her classes, the hotel, or her house. This whole fake engagement was ridiculous.

And yet she couldn't get herself to call it off. To call Tyler and tell him they could just break up now. His family didn't need to come for the holidays to meet her. It all seemed like such a waste.

But he said nothing the next day, nor the next. Days became a week, which became a month, and before she knew it, she was making macaroni salad to go with Stacey's kalua turkey and traditional Hawaiian sides of sticky rice, poi, and roasted potatoes. The Thanksgiving feast at her bed and breakfast was legendary, and she sold twenty extra seats.

Tawny had been able to get her and Tyler both a spot at the table, if only she would bring her famous macaroni salad and make four pumpkin pies.

Tawny hated pumpkin pie with a passion, but in order to celebrate the holiday with her friends—and Tyler— she'd deal with the dreaded squash. It was easier working in Stacey's big kitchen at the B&B, that was for sure.

She only wore the diamond ring when she went out with Tyler, and she still hadn't gotten used to the look or weight of it on her hand. She'd shown it to all the girls in the Women's Beach Club, as they all knew about her history with Omar and could understand why she'd made up the engagement.

She'd sworn them to secrecy, and she didn't worry about them talking to anyone. Anyone she might've been worried about had left the island a couple of weeks ago, even the dark-haired man Tawny was sure would stick around until she or Tyler slipped up.

Omar had not left the island, and he was really starting to annoy Tawny. So she mixed mayonnaise and noodles, with slivered carrots and salt, to make the best macaroni salad on the island. Stacey had told her once that she should package it and sell it, but Tawny couldn't imagine a worse life. In fact, she couldn't wash her hands fast enough after putting the gallons and gallons of salad in the fridge.

Stacey came through the door of her kitchen. "Oh, Tawny. Thank goodness."

Tawny dried her hands. "Thank goodness?" She checked on the pie shells in the oven. They seemed a little blonde still, so she set the timer for another minute and faced her friend.

Stacey glanced around, an almost guilty glint on her face. "I just wasn't sure if you were here and started on the salad yet."

"All finished." She gestured to the industrial sized fridge. "Chilling. I'm about to start on the pie filling."

A broad smile swept across her friend's face. "Great. And Sasha is almost here with the stuff to make the drinks." She looked around the kitchen. "I'll have her put them over here." She indicated a stainless steel table that was mostly clear.

"Is she bringing the syrups and flavored creams?"

"Sure is."

Sasha, another member of the Women's Beach Club, owned The Straw. The only reason Tawny bought drinks from Two Coconuts and not The Straw was the location. Sasha's stand served the other curve in the bay, and she did great over there, just like Mo did fine over on this more southern side.

Tawny's mouth watered just thinking about the specialty drinks that would be served with the meal. She measured spices and pumpkin before adding a few eggs.

"Oh, and Tyler's here."

She slopped some of the pie filling out of the bowl. "Smooth, Stacey."

"He's early." Her friend wore a look that said she wanted details. And it just so happened that Tawny had been getting less and less sleep as she spent hours thinking about Tyler, and what to do, and how to act, and what might happen in a few weeks when his parents came.

"How are things going with him?" Stacey pressed.

"We're not together."

"You're wearing his diamond ring."

Tawny glanced down at it. "Because we'll be in public today." So maybe her voice had strayed into the high range. Maybe she didn't even believe herself.

"You like him." Stacey came up beside her and stilled the hand she whisked with.

"Of course I like him." Tawny was tired of denying it, and she still had weeks to go. "I like him a lot. I like holding his hand. And kissing him...wow." She shook her head and went back to the pie filling. "But we haven't kissed in a while. He brushes his lips against my temple, stuff like that."

"Why doesn't he?"

Tawny gave Stacey a sour look. "No reason to now that the reporters are gone, right?"

Stacey took a few steps away. "So this has become real for you."

"No," Tawny said quickly.

"Tawny."

"No, all right?" Tawny hated lying to Stacey, and even worse, she didn't like that she might be lying to herself. She didn't really know how she felt about Tyler, because she couldn't separate what was real from what wasn't.

Thankfully, the door opened and Sasha came in carrying a case of flavored syrups. "More in the car," she said.

"I'll help." Tawny abandoned the pie filling and left Stacey standing in the kitchen. All the soda supplies got brought in, and the pies finished, and a few hours later, the tables which had been set up in the garden were laden with food and people.

The centerpiece of the meal came out of the *imo*, an underground oven Stacey had right on her property.

Tawny kept busy setting out the food and making sure guests got the drinks and desserts they wanted.

Only then did she turn her attention toward where the sexy, bashful billionaire stood near the trees. She approached him, feeling quite shy herself. "You wanna eat?" She threaded the fingers of both hands through his.

He grinned lazily down at her, and if they'd been dating for real, she imagined they'd share a slow kiss and then go get their Thanksgiving turkey. As it was, he said, "Yeah," and walked over to the table to get a plate.

The atmosphere was lively, with laughter and lots of talking. Tawny let herself get swept up in it, and she drank more grape lime soda than any one person should. As the pie started to disappear and Tawny sensed some guests would start to leave, Stacey jumped up and pulled out her phone and started filming.

"I want to get everyone," she said. "Wave, oh, yes, hold up a bite of pie." She laughed and moved around the table, and the crowd really got a rise out of a couple who was on the island celebrating their first anniversary as they kissed.

"Oh, and this next couple is engaged," Stacey said as she pointed the camera at Tawny and Tyler, her voice too loud, and the guests whooped. "You guys should kiss too."

Tawny's emotions went bananas. She desperately wanted to kiss him, but not like this. She tried to laugh, but it came out as more of a squawk.

Tyler chuckled, then he faced Tawny, a definite devilish glint in his eye. He smiled and pressed his lips to hers in a chaste peck.

"Boo," Stacey said, peeking out from behind the camera. "Try again."

"Stacey," Tawny warned. Her lips still tingled from the quick union with Tyler's, and he'd definitely stoked a fire inside her with the simple touch.

"Come on, come on."

Tawny wasn't sure if Stacey was trying to do her a favor or not.

"It's all right," Tyler whispered, his mouth too close to her ear. A shiver passed down her spine, especially when his hand came up to caress her bare shoulder. She'd never been happier for the mustard yellow tank top so their skin could touch.

She faced him, finding him so close, so close, too close. "It is?"

He gave a tiny shrug and then kissed her. Tawny was aware of the cheering around them, and a smile zinged through her whole body.

She wasn't sure if she was still pretending, and if Tyler was, he was very, very good at it. But she suddenly had a lot more to be grateful for on this Thanksgiving Day.

ELEVEN

TYLER PORED over the email Jason had sent about Omar. Again. It was a couple of weeks old, and he had the information memorized.

Omar didn't just deal with avocados, though the crop was his main source of income. Jason's report didn't come right out and say Omar grew and distributed marijuana, but Tyler could read between the lines.

And he didn't want the man anywhere near Tawny.

He'd told her that Omar had left the island, but that wasn't true. He'd just disappeared into a mansion set behind a gate and up a long road. Jasper lived on the same side of the hill, and Tyler had asked him about the house in question.

Jasper didn't know much about it, because well, the man worked odd hours, sleeping most of the day and working with his diamond companies and mines overseas in different time zones.

Tyler kept his eye on Tawny's classes from afar, not wanting her to think he was stalking her, and he hadn't seen anyone suspicious hanging around. He probably had nothing to worry about. But why Omar was still in Getaway Bay after almost two months when he'd said he'd only be there for a couple of weeks was concerning to Tyler.

The only reason he could fathom why Omar hadn't gone back to his operations in Mexico was Tawny. According to her, the relationship was long over—years ago—but Tyler had seen the possessive edge in Omar's eyes, and he wasn't convinced a wedding ring mattered much to the man.

He finally closed the email, glad he'd gone along with the engagement. His heart pumped out an extra beat, but he ignored it. He'd been doing that a lot lately, because he didn't want to acknowledge that his family would be here in twelve days, and after their two weeks in the tropics, he'd have to really decide what to do about Tawny.

As he dressed to surf, zipping his wetsuit and sorting through his boards for the one he wanted, he could recognize that he liked the woman. A lot. A whole lot. She was tan, trim, and toned, and he'd allowed himself to hold her hand, hold her close, and kiss her even when there weren't cameras or witnesses.

She hadn't said anything, and he'd spent way too many nights wondering if she could possibly like him as more than just a buffer between her and Omar.

Of course she does, Tyler thought. She hadn't asked about him since Tyler had fibbed about him leaving the island. But there was still that niggling doubt in the back of his mind, because she resisted things like kissing him for her friend's video at Thanksgiving and coming over to help him decorate his Christmas tree.

Because she'd declined that activity, he still hadn't done it.

I will today, he told himself as he crossed the sand. He didn't need to impress his family, but he wanted them to have a traditional Hawaiian Christmas, and that meant a tree, stockings for everyone, and gifts. He'd hang lights on his house too, and in the back yard leading to the beach.

He let his troubles and worries and doubts wash away in the ocean, grateful for his life here. When he'd first decided to sell his half of the company, he hadn't thought he'd leave New York. But it became obvious to him after the deal had closed that he'd need to.

Get far away from anyone who knew much about him. He'd considered Alaska, but just because it was remote didn't mean it was easy to hide. In Getaway Bay, he could easily blend in as there were thousands and thousands of tourists in and out every week.

His surfing complete and after he showered, he set to work on decorating the house. He even turned on some Hawaiian Christmas music as he trimmed the tree and wrapped the few things he'd already bought for his family. Tawny had been with him and given him great advice on the pearls for his mother, the more souvenier-like shirts and flip flops for his nephews, and the loud Hawaiian shirt for his father.

He didn't have anything for Wayne or his wife, Gina,

but there was still plenty of time to shop. Truth was, he'd only met Gina once, when she and Wayne had gotten married seven years ago. He'd moved to Hawaii soon after that, and while he kept in touch with his brother on a regular basis, he didn't talk to Gina all that much.

By mid-afternoon, he had the most Christmasy house on the block, and he stood on the street in front of his house and admired his handiwork.

He turned as movement caught in his peripheral vision to find Tawny riding toward him on her bicycle. A smile sprang to his face at the sight of her, and his heart did that extra bump thing, reminding him that maybe the only fake thing about their relationship was the diamond she wore.

"There you are." She dismounted and leaned her bike against one of the trees he'd just spent thirty minutes covering in lights. "I've called you a couple of times."

He couldn't help the way his whole soul felt uplifted by those simple words. "Miss me that much?" He grinned and took her into his arms. She smelled like tanning lotion, and sand, and sunshine, and he loved the way her scent filled his nose.

"Very funny."

"What's funny about it?" He'd already said a few things that she could've interpreted as *hey, I really like you, and maybe we should keep seeing each other after Christmas*. But she hadn't said anything, and Tyler hadn't figured out how to either.

"You were supposed to meet me at Sweet Breeze for their tree lighting festival."

Tyler jumped back from her. "That was today?" No, he

couldn't miss that. He'd told Fisher he'd be there, not only to support a good friend, but to do a few card tricks as part of the festivities.

"Yes, that was today." Tawny looked up at him with concern. "What's going on with you?'

"Nothing," he said. "I got it into my head to decorate the house today, and I just forgot." He gestured to her bike. "You want to leave this here and we'll take my car over?"

She softened, and Tyler wanted nothing more than to kiss her. But there was no one around, not even the breeze was whispering at the moment.

The perfect time then, he thought just before leaning down and touching his lips to hers. Exploring, seeking, asking. Confessing.

She kissed him back, and Tyler wondered if he could tell her how he really felt. He'd just put his hands on her back to knead her closer, kiss her deeper, when she pulled away.

"What was that for?" she asked, cinching her arms across her chest.

"Maybe I was the one missing you," he said. That wasn't even close to what he wanted to say, but the conflicted, confused look on Tawny's face kept the rest silent.

"I don't think you should do that." She turned and walked toward the car. "And yes, I'd love a ride."

Do what? he wondered. Miss her? Or kiss her? Both, probably. He'd promised her a night at the gala, no strings attached, and that was what she obviously wanted.

His chest stung like someone had attached his heart to

a set of jumper cables, but he pushed the hurt feelings away. He joined her in the car and said, "I'm sorry. It won't happen again."

She didn't speak until he left his neighborhood, and then she said, "I know you hired Jason Barnes to look into Omar."

His muscles froze and he almost drove right off the road. Straightening out the car, he said, "I just wanted to know what I was dealing with."

"*You* don't need to deal with anything."

He glanced at her. "You're joking, right?"

"I am not."

"You made up a fake engagement because of him. A five-minute conversation with him." Tyler clenched his fingers around the steering wheel. "I have my family coming into town, and I'm trying to...make sure the holiday is special for them, and keep you safe, and...."

Stop myself from falling in love with you.

Oh, couldn't say that. He wanted to, but he bit the words back until they slithered down his throat where they belonged.

"And what?" she pressed, really striking for the bullseye whether she knew it or not.

"And now I've forgotten about Fisher's celebration," he said lamely. "I only asked Jason to look into Omar so I would have a better and bigger picture of him."

"You should've asked me."

He nodded as he turned onto the main road that ran in front of Fisher's hotel. "You're right. But I'm guessing you don't know everything Jason was able to find out."

"Why would you think I don't know?"

"You're too nice, Tawny. You trust everyone, and you're...happy."

"I'm happy?"

This wasn't going well, and Tyler sighed. "You know what I mean."

"I have no idea what you mean."

He pulled into the drive that led to the front doors of the hotel and put the car in park. "I just mean that you're wonderful. Kind." He brushed her hair off the side of her face, another indication that he had soft feelings for her that went beyond the falseness of their relationship. "He probably didn't tell you everything he did, and you didn't ask. Because you don't even think to ask. You assume everyone is good, like you are."

She gazed at him, her eyes halfway between blazing with anger and appreciation for the compliments he was trying to give her. "I also think it's weird you hired the reporter we've been trying to con to find out about Omar's shady business dealings."

Tyler shrugged. "Jason's not a bad guy. He writes for a poker magazine now, but he's been a cop and a private detective before. He's good at finding out what no one else can."

She lifted her eyebrows. "Exactly. So giving him extra access to you—to me—you thought that was a good idea?"

"Did he talk to you?" Obviously, he had. How else would she have found out about Tyler's interest in Omar?

"He sent us both an email. It had Omar's travel itinerary in it. I emailed him back to find out why he was sending me that information, and he said he assumed you'd kept me up-to-date on Omar and his 'situation'."

Tyler took her hand in his. "Did he tell you he's still on the island?"

"I gathered that from the itinerary."

"And that's when you hopped on your bike and rode to my place."

"No, then I came here, because I thought we were meeting here, and I didn't want to miss the tree lighting."

Another shot of guilt hit Tyler in the gut. He didn't know what to say, though words streamed through his mind.

She exhaled and said, "I'm not mad. But can we be honest with each other?"

Tyler looked at her, really searched her eyes. "There's nothing I want more," he said, the truth bubbling and boiling beneath his vocal chords. *You're beautiful* came to mind. *I want to kiss you even when no one's watching.*

"Great." She gave him a soft smile and leaned back against the headrest. "Because I don't think you're dressed appropriately for even card tricks."

He glanced down at his faded yellow T-shirt and board shorts. "Well, why didn't you say so when I was still at home?"

She laughed, and Tyler caught the movement of the valet as he came toward the car. He still leaned over and silenced the laughter coming from Tawny's mouth by covering hers with his. This kiss wasn't nearly as soft as the one outside his house, but she didn't seem to mind. In fact, she slung one hand around the back of his neck and kissed him back.

Passionately.

The door opened behind him, and then the valet said, "Oh, excuse me," and shut the door again.

Tyler rested his forehead against Tawny's, the weight of her arm across his shoulders sensual and spine-tingling. "Honestly?" he whispered, hoping he wasn't about to make the biggest mistake of his life. "I think this fake relationship has gotten a little too real for me."

Before she could answer, he untangled himself from her and got out of the car. Sterling stood there, his face the color of Tawny's cherry soda.

"I'm sorry, sir," he said stiffly.

"It's fine, Sterling." Tyler slipped him some money. "Did I miss too much of the festival?"

"It's still going strong, sir."

"Great." Tyler watched as Tawny unfolded herself from his low profile sports car, and wow, she was the most radiant woman he'd ever laid eyes on. Her gaze locked with his, and he wasn't entirely sure since it had been a while since he'd dated anyone, but she looked like she had fire in the blue depths of her eyes.

Now, whether that was angry fire or passionate fire, he wasn't sure. Both would burn him, and he hoped he was ready for the heat.

TWELVE

HE'D DONE IT AGAIN. Tyler had said something that had Tawny topsy-turvy and not sure what the heck was going on.

Did he like that their relationship was too real? Or was he upset about it and wanted to pull back? See her less? Kiss her never again?

Because the man kissed her like she was his dying breath, and she felt herself slipping down a slope toward loving him quickly. So he'd done some private investigating on Omar. He was probably right that the avocado grower did more than Tawny knew.

And though he wore his beach clothes, she still felt like a princess walking on his arm into the hotel, which now sported a huge, twenty-five-foot Christmas tree in the lobby on the first floor.

"Holy cow." Tyler paused and drank in the tree before him, a smile spreading across his handsome face. The tree had ornaments of all sizes, from great big gold balls to small ceramic surfboards. Whoever Fisher had commissioned to do the tree had taken the charm and exactly what Getaway Bay stood for and turned it into Christmas decorations.

The multi-colored lights seemed to brighten the lobby, though it was broad daylight and the sun threw it's light everywhere.

"It's pretty, isn't it?"

"Beautiful." He turned and looked at her, something raw on his face. She'd seen this look in the car on the way over too, and she wanted to know what it meant.

"Are you going to stand me up for the parade tonight?" She quirked one eyebrow at him, and he chuckled.

"I don't think you're leaving my sight for the rest of the day." He pulled her closer and pressed his lips to her temple, a gesture he'd done many times since the gala, and each time it made Tawny feel more treasured, more adored, more loved.

Which was stupid, really. But she couldn't help how she felt. She'd been looking for a man like Tyler for years, and she couldn't believe he'd been right there, a half a mile from her house, all this time.

And he *had* asked her to the gala.

They moved toward and past the tree to the activities beyond it. "Why did you ask me?" she asked, feeling brave and maybe a little reckless. "I mean, if we're going to be honest and all that, why did you ask me to the gala?"

Before he could answer, Owen Church, the general manager of Sweet Breeze, approached and said, "Tyler.

Mister DuPont would like to see you." He cut a glance at Tawny. "Hello, Miss Loveless."

"Owen, have you seen Stacey?"

"She's at pool eight," Owen said without missing a beat. "She said if I saw you to send you up." He half-turned and gestured for Tyler to go with him. "Tyler, please. Fisher says it's quite important."

Tawny exchanged a glance with Tyler. "Guess I'll be out of your sight for a while." She added a smile to the statement so he would know she was teasing him.

"And I left my phone at home," he said, a blip of anxiety slipping through his eyes.

"You can call the pool," Owen said.

Tyler hesitated yet another moment, and then he stepped close, cupped her face in one hand and kissed her. This was a completely different kind of kiss than the one in the car. That had felt heated, almost desperate. This was sweet, kind, and slow, and Tyler didn't seem to mind that there were hundreds of people teeming around them.

In fact, that was probably why he was kissing her right now. So everyone could see.

"I'll see you soon, okay?" His whispered words almost sounded like a plea, and definitely didn't come off as a man who was simply fulfilling his word. No, he sounded like he could actually like her.

Dazed and in disbelief, she watched him walk away, his head bent close with Owen's. They disappeared down a private hallway that Tawny knew went to Fisher's office.

Sighing, she turned as if she'd have a best friend standing right behind her to gush about Tyler with. But

Esther wasn't there, and Stacey was waiting at pool eight on the twenty-sixth floor.

As Tawny went to the elevator and ascended toward the pool, she had the sinking feeling that she was already in love with Tyler Rigby, and that when the holidays ended, she'd lose her heart all over again.

———

Tawny found Stacey, Esther, Sasha, and Winnie at pool eight. All members of the Women's Beach Club, the women were sunbathing with sodas nearby. None of them seemed to be talking, so Tawny simply sat in the only lounger left and kicked off her sandals.

A waitress appeared and Tawny ordered a mango pineapple mocktail, with a side of chips and salsa.

That got Esther's attention. "Chips and salsa?" She peered over her mirrored sunglasses, her blonde hair wisping with a sudden uptick in the breeze.

"I didn't eat lunch," Tawny said.

"Too worried about Tyler?"

"Something like that." Tawny pulled her sunglasses out of her bag and slipped them on. She wasn't wearing a bathing suit, but her tank and shorts were just fine for lying in the sun.

"Did you find him?" Stacey asked.

"Yeah, he was just at home. He said he forgot."

"Mm."

Sasha turned her head and squinted at Tawny. "What's going to happen with you guys?"

"What do you mean?"

"What she means," Esther said. "Is that it's obvious that you've fallen for him."

"No, I haven't." Tawny wished she had her big drink to hide behind. "We both knew the situation going in."

Esther scoffed, but it was Stacey who said, "That doesn't mean you haven't fallen for him."

"That's exactly what it means," Tawny said. "Help me out here, Winnie."

"Oh, girl," the woman said. "Even I can see you like him."

"Liking him and falling for him are two different things. He's a great guy. He's become a friend. Nothing wrong with that."

Stacey finally sat up and reached for her bag. She withdrew her phone and passed it to Winnie. "Check out the third video."

"Stacey," Tawny warned, but Winnie started tapping and scrolling anyway. There was no sound, but Tawny didn't need to hear it to know what Winnie was seeing. The video from Thanksgiving dinner at Aloha Hideaway.

"Mm hm." Winnie passed the phone to Tawny, nothing else to say, apparently.

Tawny took the device but she didn't look at it. She had a feeling she'd both like what she saw and be utterly horrified. Her drink came, along with her chips and salsa, and she busied herself with them so she wouldn't have to try to defend herself against what was obvious to her friends.

Was it obvious to Tyler too?

She stuffed another salsa-laden chip in her mouth, but it was really hard to swallow.

"Okay," she finally said. "What am I going to do?"

Sasha gave her a sympathetic look, but Esther and Stacey both started laughing. Tawny let them have their fun, and then she said, "Seriously, guys."

"Have you thought about telling him the truth?" Stacey asked.

She thought about their vow to be honest with each other. She wasn't sure she could stomach the thought of losing him. *You're going to lose him anyway.*

"And say what? 'Hey, I know this started out as a ruse, but I've fallen for you, and I'd like to…to…I don't even know what!" Frustration built inside Tawny's chest, making breathing difficult.

"You want to keep seeing him," Esther said. "Dating him. After his family's gone."

"But what if he doesn't feel the same?" She couldn't do that to him, not a week and a half before his family came to town. She wouldn't. He'd been nothing but kind to her, and she liked almost everything about him. Sure, his nonchalance about his money was a little odd, as was his seeming overprotectiveness of her. She didn't like that he'd hired someone to look into Omar and hadn't told her.

But other than that, he was darn near perfect. And not only that, but perfect for her.

She groaned and closed her eyes, wishing she could just float away into the sunshine, no cares or worries in the world weighing her down.

"Honey," Winnie said. "I don't want another man. But you do. I know you do. You always have."

Tawny nodded, too mentally exhausted to smile at Winnie, who really was a great friend. "Thanks, Winnie."

"Maybe he's the one. Maybe it'll take something hard to keep him," she said. "And I've never known you to shy away from doing something hard."

Tawny nodded again, but the words rolled around in her head and took root.

Maybe he's the one.

Tell him the truth.

It'll take something hard to keep him.

"I'll talk to him after Christmas," she murmured. Perhaps none of her friends heard her. Or perhaps they didn't believe her, just like she didn't believe herself. After all, having a fake relationship with Tyler was better than none at all, and Tawny was sure if she told him the truth, she'd lose him. She'd confessed feelings for men too soon before, and she wasn't going to repeat that mistake here.

Nope. Her resolve to do everything the opposite as she normally did hardened, and she let her thoughts drift. So he'd said a few things that had confused her. But that was because she was trying to hear something in his words that wasn't there.

THIRTEEN

TYLER LISTENED as Fisher went through the accommodations for his family. They'd been booked into the penthouse on the twenty-seventh floor, just one level below Fisher. He'd said several times already that he'd attend to anything they needed personally.

The penthouse didn't take up the whole footprint the way Fisher's did, but the three bed-room unit was three times as big as Tyler's house, with the nicest furnishings, a full kitchen, and three bathrooms.

"They'll be fine," he'd told Fisher, but the man insisted on walking through the welcome package, the amenities included, all of it. He finally finished, and Tyler wondered how he'd ever worked as hard as Fisher.

He had, in the past. Poker was ninety percent skill and ten percent luck. His photographic memory helped immensely as he studied his opponents, counted cards, and learned the best combinations to win. Sometimes a two could beat an ace, and he knew all the ways that could happen.

His nerves of steel took care of the rest. When he felt like calling, he bid instead. When the guy across from him flinched, he doubled-down. Tyler had worked and traveled, barely taking time to eat or sleep, once. And he never wanted to be like that again.

"So let's talk about you and Tawny," Fisher said next, and that got Tyler to sit up straighter. He cut a glance at Owen, who didn't act like he'd heard a word. He continued to tap away on his computer, squinting at something and then looking at a ledger in front of him.

"What about her?" Tyler asked.

"I need to inform my staff about the relationship. Make sure no one slips up."

"Slips up about what? And aren't you personally attending to my family?" He looked at Owen again, somehow wanting the man to confirm.

"They could come in contact with any number of people," Fisher said.

"All of whom think Tawny and I are engaged," Tyler said. "I don't see the problem."

"Fisher was talking too loudly to Marshall about it," Owen said, still pecking away at his work. "A few people overheard."

Fear struck Tyler right behind his breastbone.

"I was not talking too loud," Fisher said, clearly cross with his GM.

"Fisher," Tyler said, so much warning in his voice it felt dangerous.

"I was in my own home," Fisher said, his eyes earnest. "Marshall was there, sure. But we both know the nature of the relationship. The door was ajar for room service, and they didn't announce themselves."

Tyler cocked his head, trying to decide how much this mattered. "You've had that problem a lot."

"Very funny." Fisher shook his head, a tiny smile appearing on his face. "I've taken care of the problem both times. But I'm wondering if I should assign those two to your family, since they already know." He flipped his phone over and over.

"I don't think it matters," Tyler said. "But maybe you shouldn't be discussing my relationship when it's none of your business."

"Your relationship?" Fisher stilled and looked right at Tyler. Even Owen stopped the incessant typing and turned to watch him.

"It's...complicated." Tyler wasn't going to say more.

Fisher exchanged a glance with Owen, and Tyler hated that they'd talked about him without his knowledge.

"Have you learned more about Omar Velasquez?" Fisher asked.

Tyler nodded. "He's not a nice guy, but he doesn't seem to be doing anything illegal here. He won't even come out of that house up in the hills."

"Have you talked to Jasper?"

"Yep. He doesn't know anything."

"Owen?"

"I will see what I can find out." The general manager had ways of learning things that maybe others couldn't.

Tyler had no idea how, or what he'd do, but it didn't matter. Knowledge was power when playing with dangerous personalities. Tyler should know. He'd made millions outsmarting the smartest players in the world.

"All right. Well, I think we're ready for your family."

"Thanks, Fisher." Tyler stood. "I'm sorry about this morning. I just got focused on something else."

He waved his hand. "It was a few card tricks. No big deal."

Tyler left his friend's office, wondering if he was welcome at pool eight with Tawny and her friends. He decided he didn't care. He wanted to spend time with her, and if that meant he had to interrupt her girl time, he'd do it.

He knew he'd made a mistake when he stepped onto the pool deck, and five pairs of female eyes traveled to him. Though he was dressed in proper pool attire, he felt like he absolutely did not belong.

Tawny lay partially back in a lounger, one leg flung over the other at the knee. She was so sexy she took his breath away and he stalled on the other side of the pool. No way he was going over there to talk to her with Stacey, Esther, Sasha, and another woman he didn't know watching him. Listening. *Eavesdropping.*

Stacey pushed her sunglasses down her nose and studied him as if she wasn't sure who he was.

He lifted his hand in a wave and pointed back the way he'd come. Then he got the heck out of there, using some of his intelligence on something other than poker for once in his life.

Since he didn't have his phone, he simply went back to the elevator, which sat outside the dressing rooms. Too much time passed before Tawny showed up, but he couldn't help smiling at her.

"So, gossiping about me with your friends?"

"Absolutely." She grinned and leaned her palms against his chest. "It was a nice nap though. What did you and Fisher talk about?"

"My family's accommodations. They're staying here."

"They are?" True surprise colored her voice.

"Well, my place is too small. The nephews might stay with me and Lazy Bones."

"But we're eating at your place, right?"

"On Christmas and Christmas Eve, yes." He put his hands on her waist, the shape of her in front of him so perfect, he couldn't stop himself from saying, "Tawny, there's something I wanted to talk to you about."

The word vomit built, built, built, and he knew he was going to blow everything up. *Don't do it*, he coached himself. *Do not say another word.*

"Sure, anything." Her fingertips slid along his collar and behind his head, where she played with the ends of his hair. His pulse went wild, and instead of talking, Tyler leaned down and kissed her.

He was sure he said more by doing that anyway. She had to know he was falling in love with her, so why couldn't he say it out loud?

———

He took Tawny to the light parade that night, enjoying some Hawaiian traditions he'd never really participated in before. Having Santa's sleigh be a canoe pulled by dolphins was a bit odd for him, but he loved the hula dancing and the ukulele music. He ate too much ice cream, and bought Tawny too many fruity drinks.

Time slipped away, and before he knew it, he'd said nothing to Tawny about how he felt about her, nothing about wanting to continue the relationship after his family left, nothing about what he wanted to talk to her about. She never asked either, and Tyler decided it was because she didn't want to perpetuate their relationship after the holidays.

He woke a few days before Christmas to Lazy Bones barking—something he never did. Dawn hadn't quite arrived yet, so Tyler sat up in bed and listened. He didn't have to strain that hard to hear the reverberation of something hitting his front door.

He launched himself out of bed and headed for the door, not caring that he only wore a pair of gym shorts. "Hey!" he yelled, glad when Lazy Bones came with him, still barking his fool head off.

Another bang and then the very distinct sound of a car roaring to life met his ears. Tyler pulled open the door expecting dripping eggs, though it wasn't Halloween nor a full moon. Nor did he live in an area with a lot of teenagers.

But it wasn't egg yolks stuck to his wood. At least it didn't look like it. No, this was greenish. He left the mess for now and leapt down the steps, hoping to catch a glimpse of the car.

It rounded a corner, and since it was still fairly dark, he couldn't tell what color it was. Could've been black, or blue, or maroon. Probably wasn't white.

His adrenaline spiking and his heart hammering, he turned back to the house. Lazy Bones sat on the front porch, licking the slop off the steps.

"Bones," he called. "No." He wanted to see what it was first, before the gluttonous dog ate it all.

He slicked some off the front door, the texture very eggy and somewhat creamier. And that green…. He sniffed it, and exclaimed, "Avocados."

Turning back to the street, his adrenaline turned the corner toward fear. Omar had thrown eggs at his house? Were they fourteen? It didn't seem like something the man would do, and his confusion doubled.

"What is that?" He pulled something from Lazy Bones's lips to find an avocado rind. The eggs had been cracked inside it, and that had been thrown at his house.

And his parents were coming today. He clenched his teeth and got to work cleaning up the mess. The last thing he needed was an avocado/drug lord terrorizing him while his family was here visiting.

He'd just gotten all the evidence of the attack erased when Tawny showed up with a big pack on her back. She'd pulled her hair up into a high ponytail and she wore a smile that made his whole world light up.

"Morning, you," she said. "I thought you'd be surfing."

"Yeah, I—yeah, I didn't go this morning."

She gave him a look like *Hmm, that's odd*, but didn't say anything. "I'm here to make the sticky rice for lunch."

"I got all the stuff you said you needed."

She trailed her fingertips up his arm, making him shiver like he had chosen Alaska as the place where he wanted to escape. "Thanks."

He turned to watch her walk by, the cute little running shorts revealing a lot of leg. With his blood pumping harder through his body, he waited until she went up the freshly swept and hosed off steps and into his house.

She had a schedule for the day, and he'd promised not to interrupt her. She was here early to make the sticky rice so she could get back in time for her class. She'd race home to shower, and then they'd go to the airport to pick up his parents.

He'd bought fifteen pounds of pulled pork and lots of buns, but she'd insisted on making the sticky rice. Called it her specialty. He liked that he was still learning things about Tawny that he didn't know after two full months of spending time together almost every day.

He kept his promise and took Lazy Bones to the beach instead of loitering in his own kitchen just to be near Tawny. He did eventually return, and her voice carried on the quietness through the open windows at the back of his house.

"…I don't know. We'll see…."

He tried to make as much noise as possible as he threw the Frisbee he and Bones had been playing with. But she continued with, "We're just friends."

Just friends.

The words tasted like poison. They sounded like bombs exploding. They stabbed like freshly sharpened knives.

Friends? he thought as she said, "Yeah, he's cute…fine, gorgeous…yes, I know."

He couldn't stand to hear anything else. He didn't want to be her gorgeous friend. He wanted so much more than that, and he was going to tell her right after his family left. He made sure to push the door closed with extra force, which brought her around from where she worked at the counter.

"Yeah, I gotta go." She hung up and set her phone on the island. "Hey, everything's looking good." She had a towel slung over her shoulder and with that cocked hip, he wanted to rush her and profess how he really felt about her.

Something invisible held him back. "Great," he said, his voice dead even to his own ears.

Tawny blinked, her brows furrowing slightly. "Everything okay?"

"Yes," he said, but he shook his head no.

"Yes? Or no?"

"I'm gonna go shower." He had to get away from her. He'd never explained why his money didn't matter to him, but it was because women expected a man with a lot of money to be the ultimate alpha. Always in control. The one barking orders and getting things done.

Tyler had been that man for a while, and he'd hated himself. He didn't want to be the top dog, the one who always had to know what to do.

And now he was the complete opposite of that. Now,

he couldn't even tell her that he'd overheard her, and it upset him, and he wanted way more than friends.

He turned around to go lay everything on the line and almost knocked her to the ground. He grabbed onto her arms to keep her from falling. "Whoa. Whoa."

"Sorry." She exhaled and found her feet beneath her. He let go of her quickly, probably faster than he ever had.

"I was just going to confirm that you're picking me up at eleven."

"I'll be there."

"My class goes until ten-thirty, but I'll be ready."

He nodded, his throat aching from how hard he was working to keep his words dormant.

She backed up a step, and his hands fell from her arms. He escaped into his bedroom, where he knew she wouldn't follow, and locked the door. He pressed his back into it, sucking at the air like it wasn't the right thing to breathe. Why did he feel like this? He'd literally never felt like this before.

Because he'd never been in love before.

———

Eleven o'clock came and Tyler parked in front of Tawny's place. She came bounding down the steps five minutes later, her hair curled and her makeup flawless. She wore a pair of strappy, white sandals with a sundress with big sunflowers on it.

His fingers flexed around the steering wheel, and his chest felt hollowed out. He was sure he wouldn't be able to speak at all, but when she got in and asked, "Did you get the leis?" he managed to squeeze out "Yeah. In the back."

She twisted to find the box of colorful flower leis he'd bought for every member of his family. Since they hadn't been to Hawaii when he lived there, he wanted to give them all the traditional and touristy things in this one trip.

He got to the airport without having to say much, thanks to a beautiful day and all the windows down.

Once they'd parked and gone into the airport, Tawny slipped her hand into his. Even with electric current rippling through him, he cocked one eyebrow at her.

"What?" she asked. "We're engaged. We should be holding hands."

"They're flight doesn't land for another fifteen minutes."

She started to pull her fingers away, but Tyler held onto them. Tight, tighter. "Or maybe you hold hands with all of your *friends*." He wasn't sure where the venom in his voice had come from, only that it was there.

She blinked at him, confusion evident on her face. "What?"

"We're just friends, right? Isn't that what you said on the phone this morning?"

Her face paled even beneath all the makeup. "You heard that?"

"I threw the Frisbee really hard," he said. "You just kept on talking." He felt like he was getting stung over and over again by a killer wasp. On his skin. Inside his mouth. His lungs. He wanted to say it was fine, that he liked her as a friend too, but his tongue had somehow swollen in his mouth. That, or he couldn't keep lying to himself—or to her.

Tawny stepped in front of him, the baggage claim and waiting area just a dozen feet away. "What's going on here?"

"Nothing." He looked over her shoulder and put on his poker face.

"Don't do that." She lifted onto her toes and moved into his line of sight. "Don't put on that blank mask. I hate that thing."

He met her eyes, and she looked as stormy as he felt. "I don't want to be called your friend. *I* hated *that*."

Something akin to hope entered her expression. Could she really want to be with him? The man behind the blank mask? The man who would've married someone he barely knew just because she'd gotten pregnant? The man who her ex-boyfriend was harassing with avocados and eggs?

"Oh, and your *friend* Omar egged my house this morning. He was good enough to throw in a few avocados so I would know it was him." Tyler searched the arrivals board and discovered that his family's plane was early. "They're here already." He wished he'd chosen a better time to hint at his true feelings for Tawny, but there was nothing he could do about it now.

FOURTEEN

TAWNY COULDN'T QUITE GET a grip on reality. *I don't want to be called your friend.*

What did he want to be called then?

Tyler turned to scan the people coming through the security exit, but she couldn't see anyone like the pictures he'd shown her.

Besides, there was so many things more important than his parents in this moment. "Omar egged your house?"

"This morning."

Tawny once again stepped in front of him, a tidal wave of concern flooding her. "Tyler, that's not good."

"Tell me about it. Shorted out some of my lights washing off the porch."

"No, it means he's marked you."

That got him to stop scanning the crowd coming out and look at her. Finally. "What does that mean?"

"It means he knows you've been digging up dirt on him, and he's not happy about it."

"What's he going to do?"

Before she could answer, a woman squealed and he jumped in front of Tawny so she wouldn't get trampled by his mother.

"Tyler!" She laughed and laughed as she hugged him, jumping up and down.

"All right, Mom. All right." He chuckled too while Tawny stood out of the way, watching this private family reunion. She almost felt like she shouldn't be there, and her first instinct was to leave.

Of course you shouldn't be here, she told herself. *This is all wrong.*

It was one thing to dupe Omar, an all-around devil of a person. But his family? His family whom he hadn't seen in six years?

He smiled as big as she'd ever seen him as his dad joined them, along with Wayne and Gina and the boys. Tyler hugged everyone and swooped the nephews into his arms at the same time.

"How was the plane? Did you guys fall asleep?"

Hudson and Darius talked for only a moment and then Tyler set them down. He let his eyes skate past Tawny's when he reached for her, and my, if that didn't dig right into her bone marrow. But she put her hand in his, right where he needed her, right when he needed her, because he'd done the same for her.

"This is Tawny Loveless, my fiancée." He indicated the six people in front of him. "Tawny, my mom, Shirley. Dad

Rich. My brother Wayne and his wife, Gina. And their two boys, Darius and Hudson."

"So nice to finally meet you," she gushed as if she'd been waiting years. "I'm so glad you could come for the holidays." She shook hands and didn't squirm under the scathing scrutiny of his family. She hated that they were on shaky ground during this crucial time, but she reminded herself that she'd put him in this position. He'd done a lot for her all these weeks leading up to this. She could perform for ten more days.

"Oh, leis." She passed them out, babbling about the tradition of the flowers, the shells, the nuts. "The lei is a symbol of love, friendship—" She cut a quick glance at Tyler, who wore that blasted poker face again "—celebration, honor, or greeting." She finished putting the last one on Wayne and stepped back. "In this case, it's all of those for you." She beamed at them, hoping they'd feel right at home on the island, in Getaway Bay.

"Well." His mom smoothed down her silk blouse, careful not to disturb her lei. "Let's go to lunch. I'm starving."

"Oh, we made lunch at the house," Tyler said. "Remember?"

His mother made a sour face and then brightened. "Oh, yes, that's right. I think Tawny was going to make sticky rice."

"That's right." She smiled at the woman, sure they'd get along just fine. But she immediately glommed onto Tyler and started whispering in his ear, leaving Tawny to walk with Gina.

"Don't let her get to you," Gina said almost under her breath.

"She's not."

"Oh, but she will." Gina gave her a knowing smile. "Just remember that you live here, and she lives in Queens. *Biiig* buffer zone."

Wayne sidled up beside Tawny and asked, "What are you two whispering about?"

"Not whispering," Gina said, an innocent smile on her face.

"Right." Wayne put the eye-rolling in his tone. "So, Tawny what do you do?"

"I'm a beach yoga instructor right now."

"Right now? You used to do something else?"

"Yeah, I've worked on cruise ships, resorts, that kind of thing." She forced a laugh out of her mouth, still watching as Tyler's mom fingered his hair, a look of displeasure on her face. If he cut it because of her…. Tawny shook the thoughts away.

"I even did life coaching for a year or so." She added a smile to her sentence, hoping Wayne and Gina didn't ask her any questions. She hadn't been particularly good at life coaching, as hers at the time had been a complete mess.

Tyler's mother turned around, her face the perfect example of someone smelling manure. She painted a smile over it, but Tawny's self-confidence took a dive. Maybe this was going to be a very long ten days after all, especially with Tyler being all mysterious and cryptic with his words.

Since he drove a tiny little sports car, his family had

rented a minivan for their stay on the island. They really looked like tourists loading their luggage in the back of the van and bickering about where each of them would sit.

They finally all loaded up, and with Wayne behind the wheel, Tawny felt sure they'd make it to Tyler's house just fine.

"Should we go?" he asked, startling her out of the trance she'd fallen into.

"Yes. Yes, let's go." She set her feet to walking, because it was almost as easy as breathing. "They're great," she said before he could ask. "What was your mom saying about your hair?"

"Oh, she's never liked my hair."

"She seemed excited to see you."

"She did, didn't she?" He smiled, and Tawny got the impression, as she had for months now, that he loved his family. They loved him. They might not be perfect, but they were family.

She had the urge to return to their conversation, the one they'd been having before his parents had arrived. But her nerves failed her, and she let him turn the radio up loud and put the windows down low, both of which made talking quite difficult.

They arrived at Tyler's house just ahead of his family, which left them no time for talking anyway.

"Look," he said just as she reached for the handle. With doubt popping through her, she turned back.

"Let's just get through this, okay?" He reached over and cupped her cheek in his palm. The touch was so intimate and sweet, Tawny closed her eyes and breathed in, hoping to hold onto the moment forever.

But it ended, as time marched on no matter what, and she caught him looking in the rear-view mirror when she opened her eyes.

"A quick kiss," he murmured.

Tawny barely had time to comprehend his words before his mouth touched hers. The heat between them still existed, even if there were unsaid things between them. She savored the taste of him, the way his mouth seemed made to mold to hers.

Someone rapped on his window, and he drew back a sigh leaking from his lips. "All right. Let's go eat lunch."

———

Tawny fluttered around Tyler's kitchen, picking up lunch dishes and serving coffee. He'd set up a picnic table in the back big enough for everyone, and with the sound of the bay waves in the background, lunch had gone well.

Well, as well as Tawny could've hoped after meeting a man's parents and trying to pass herself off as their son's fiancée.

She brought out the chocolate cake he'd bought that morning while she'd been teaching, and the last two coffee cups. With everything on the table, she said, "Who wants cake?"

"Oh, not me," Shirley said. "Too much sugar, and after that long flight and that heavy food." She waved her hand like chocolate cake was made of mud.

Everyone else seemed just fine after the flight and the "heavy food." So Tawny served up the cake and then settled with her coffee, no cake in front of her either.

"So," Shirley said. "You two still don't have a date set?"

"Mom," Tyler said. "I told you we didn't."

"I know, but that was two months ago." She pinned him with a look before switching it to Tawny. "Things change, right?"

Tawny gave her a closed-mouth smile and lifted her coffee mug again. Things certainly did change, and in the two months since he'd "announced" his engagement to his parents, she'd fallen in love with him.

Stupid, stupid thing to do.

"No date," Tyler said. "We're just playing it by ear."

Shirley scoffed, as if no one played anything by ear these days. "Well, we'll need time to plan."

"Mom," Tyler said, throwing a desperate look at Tawny. But what did he expect her to do? "*You* don't need to plan anything. Tawny and I are more than capable. We don't want anything big anyway, and it'll probably be right here." He indicated the beach in front of him, and Tawny almost swooned at the very idea of becoming his bride on this stretch of sand.

She could already see it: Tea lights in the palm trees. Music playing from the branches. The sound of the ocean in the background. A few rows of white chairs, and her, and Tyler, and everyone they cared about....

A blissful sigh escaped her lips, and Tyler's gaze shot to her. His eyebrows lifted as if to say, *What?* but she just shook her head.

A fool's fantasy, that was what she was imagining.

"We'll need time to buy tickets," she said, her voice slightly wounded.

"Mom, I can buy you a ticket any time you want."

"I can too, Mom," Wayne said, which earned him a glare from Shirley.

"Humph." She folded her arms and watched her two grandsons play in the sand nearby. Tawny was just beginning to relax when Shirley said, "What about kids?"

Tawny choked, the sip of coffee she'd just taken making a reappearance.

"Mom," Wayne chastised, clearly trying to help his brother.

"What?" Shirley looked around the table, and Rich seemed bent on watching the boys every move. He seemed oblivious to the conversation. "Is it wrong of me to want more grandchildren? You and Gina said you're done, and we don't even have any girls yet." She looked between Tyler and Tawny. "You two want kids, don't you?"

"Of course," Tawny said. She suspected she'd say anything to appease Shirley at this point.

"No," Tyler said.

Her gaze whipped to his, and it was blatantly obvious that they hadn't talked about this before. And why would they? This wasn't a real relationship. She didn't need to know his thoughts on having children, just like he didn't need to know who she'd been before she started doing everything backward.

"Oh, I see I've touched a nerve." Shirley seemed quite

satisfied with herself, and Tawny was hoping someone else would ask another question.

She wasn't expecting it to be Tyler. "You want kids?"

"You don't?" Tawny could throw his attitude right back at him. Of course she'd never told him that one of the reasons she felt so hopeless was because the longer it took her to find the right man for her, the faster her biological clock ticked.

"I've always wanted to be a mother," she said quietly, almost reverently, like they were alone and she was confiding in him. She met Shirley's eye. "But I can't promise you girls. That, I believe, is up to him." She hooked her thumb at Tyler, the very thought of sleeping with him making her flushed.

She stood, suddenly needing a break. "Who needs more coffee?"

Gina stood too and took Wayne's cup though he said, "I've barely had any."

"Well, this is cold," she said before ushering Tawny into the house. With the door closed, a particle of relief seeped into her bones.

"Thank you," Tawny said.

"Oh, I'm well-acquainted with Shirley." She poured herself more coffee and dumped Wayne's down the sink before facing Tawny. "Be straight with me. I'm not his brother or his parents. I like you. You have a good air about you. I just need you to answer one question."

Tawny's heart rippled like a flag in a stiff breeze. "What do you want to know?" She wanted to press her eyes closed and pray, but she maintained eye contact with Gina instead.

The woman had dark, wavy hair that fell halfway down her back. Her dark eyes didn't leave Tawny as she began braiding, and she didn't speak until her hair was knotted on top of her head.

"You're not doing this for his money, are you?"

Tawny was supremely glad she hadn't taken another drink of coffee. She'd have spit it out too. A laugh flowed from her easily, and she said, "No. I don't care about his money." As she said it, she realized how true it was. She'd never understood how he couldn't care about money, but she got it now.

Money couldn't get her what she wanted. Sure, it made some things easier. But no amount of money on the earth could buy her the bravery she needed to have a hard conversation with Tyler.

His money couldn't get him what he wanted either. He'd hinted at his past life, other women, the parties surrounding the poker tournaments. She didn't understand all of it, and she didn't want to.

But she knew something about him now she hadn't before. His huge amount of money couldn't buy him what he wanted on the mainland. So he'd come to Hawaii, to Getaway Bay, and found his own brand of happiness.

And it was a golden retriever, a one-bedroom beach house, and the ability to surf his morning hours away.

His happiness didn't include a woman—it hadn't for six long years—and Tawny was deluding herself if she thought he needed her at all.

FIFTEEN

TYLER STARED past his father's shoulder while his mother talked and talked and talked. So she didn't like Tawny, and Tyler couldn't fathom why.

He finally said, "Mom, stop."

"You said you wouldn't do this," Wayne added, and the two brothers exchanged a glance.

"Do what?" His mom looked back and forth between the three men at the table, but his dad was so engrossed with the sand castle the little boys were building. Wayne rolled his eyes, and Tyler heaved a sigh.

"You've said four words to her," Tyler said. "You haven't even tried to like her."

"She's just not for you." She lifted her chin—and her nose—in the air. "Did you know she was a life coach?"

Tyler had not known that little tidbit, but it hardly mattered. "Mom, she teaches beach yoga at the ritziest hotel in the bay."

"Yoga." She scoffed. "That's not a job."

"That's funny. I've seen her go to work and get paid. Seems like a job." And it was more than he'd done in years, maybe ever. Playing poker—was that a job? How was it any better than what Tawny did?

"She's beneath you."

He shook his head, unwilling to continue this argument. "She's my fiancée. I expect you to be nice to her."

"I am nothing but nice." His mom's voice was wounded, but Tyler didn't buy her act. She wasn't nearly as good as Tawny, though they were both putting on quite the show.

He stared past his nephews to the water, the siren's call of it loud in his ears, his soul. He wished he hadn't had to skip his morning surf that day, and while he'd been anticipating his family's arrival, he sort of wished they were gone already.

"Well, should we get over to the hotel?" His dad finally turned and joined the conversation. "With the time difference, it's about eight o'clock in New York."

"Oh, yeah, sure." Tyler practically leapt to his feet. His dad picked up his coffee cup as well as his mother's.

"We can clean up later," Tyler told him.

"I can take in my own coffee cup." His dad gave him a quick smile that had some sympathy stitched into it. Wayne picked up a few errant napkins and the chocolate cake plates. Tyler took the cake, noting that his mother brought in herself, the little boys, and a single fork. He decided it was something, and he couldn't be mad for the next ten days.

Inside the kitchen, Gina laughed at something, and Tyler relaxed a little. Tawny *was* likeable; his mother had simply already decided not to like her.

"We're heading to the hotel," Wayne said, causing Gina to turn.

"Good idea. I'm beat."

"Fisher's got you guys in a great penthouse," Tyler said. "Has those thick blackout curtains and everything." He contemplated whether he needed to go over to the hotel with them. Make an appearance. Introduce Fisher and Owen. Probably.

Purses got gathered, and sand brushed from little boys' arms, and everyone trooped outside to load into the minivan. Tawny hung back, leaning in the doorway, and Tyler helped his nephews in and made sure everyone had everything.

"So tomorrow, we're headed to the pineapple plantations," he said. "Is that still on?"

"Yes," came several voices.

"What time is the tour?" his mom asked.

"Nine," Tyler said. "But my friend owns it. We can do whatever." Tawny wouldn't like the change in schedule, but at the moment, it was the least of his concerns.

"Nine should be fine." She peered at him. "Do you know all the richest men on the island?"

"And the richest women too, Mom." He rolled his eyes and tapped on the roof of the minivan. "I'll meet you over there." He backed up and let them roll out first. They'd need to park in the garage, not with the valet, and get all their bags. Though Fisher had people to do that, Tyler knew his dad wouldn't want to tip them. Which was ridiculous. They had plenty of money. And if they didn't, Wayne certainly did.

He glanced back to Tawny, who now sat on the top step with Lazy Bones at her side. The dog practically cuddled into her, the traitor.

"I'm going to go over there with them," he said. "Do you want to come?"

"No, you go. I'll clean up here."

He wanted to tell her she didn't need to do that. That she wasn't his maid. That he'd like her to come so they could talk. But at the same time, he needed some time to himself, to figure out what to say to her, how to fix what he'd said, how to get his mother's words out of his head.

She's beneath you.

Tyler pushed the words from his mind. He'd never once thought of himself as superior to Tawny. And honestly, he'd thought a lot about doing more than kissing with her, but if his mother knew that was what came to mind when she said *beneath*....

He pushed those thoughts from his head too. The island suddenly seemed so small, and he arrived at Sweet Breeze in only minutes. He loitered near the lobby until his loud Queens family arrived. They did make him smile, especially the nephews and Wayne.

"This way." He took them past the front desk and down the hall toward Owen's office. Tyler had texted ahead, and Owen had said to bring them back. He knocked on the door a couple of times before entering.

Both Owen and Fisher rose from their seats, nothing

but pure hospitality smiles on their faces. Introductions were made, and keys set up, WiFi passwords given out, and the code to the private elevator only Fisher used provided.

With his family taken care of, Tyler left the hotel. But he didn't collect his car from the valet, not yet. He stood on the pool deck on the twenty-seventh floor, looking out over the bay. It was a spectacular sight, with jungles and palms, water and waves, sky and sand.

For a moment, he felt the echoes of his old life. The one where he filled his day with everything and nothing, showed up to his Nine-0 meetings if he felt like it, and went to dinner every night.

Tawny had turned everything upside down, and Tyler hadn't realized how lonely and pathetic his life had been before her.

So why didn't he want to go talk to her alone, now, when he could? He'd never minded spending his time with her or sharing his space. He'd looked forward to seeing her every day, loved holding her hand, enjoyed kissing her, and…didn't want to stop doing any of those things.

He turned from the view and headed back to his car. Sterling fetched the car and asked, "Where's Tawny today?"

"Oh, my parents came in."

Sterling tilted his head slightly, and Tyler realized his answer made no sense when he said, "She didn't want to meet them?"

"No. I mean, yes. She met them. She's at my place." Tyler gave Sterling a smile, but the man didn't return it.

He held out Tyler's keys and added, "I've known her for a while," he said. "She seems happy with you."

Tyler paused, unsure of what to do with this conversation. He didn't normally have personal talks with Fisher's valet, though he'd known Sterling since the day Sweet Breeze opened.

He studied Sterling and his years in the poker seat showed him a lot more than he wanted to know. And his time at the table had also taught him how to mask everything behind a straight face or a smile.

So he grinned at Sterling and took the keys. "Thank you, Sterling. I'm pretty happy with her too."

He went back to his house on the beach, expecting to find Tawny lying in his hammock. But she wasn't there. His kitchen was spotless, all the dishes either washed or in the dishwasher, which was running.

The picnic table in the back had been cleared, and the hammock swung only in the slight breeze not because the woman he wanted to see was there.

He couldn't figure out how he went from hot to cold and back so fast. He wanted to see her, he didn't want to see her.

But he knew he didn't like coming back to his house and being alone. Even Lazy Bones wasn't there to greet him, and he whistled to call the dog.

His phone chimed at that moment, almost an answer to his call.

Chocolate cake in the fridge. And Bones wanted to come with me, so I let him. Hope that's okay.

No mention of seeing him later, or when she'd bring Bones back. She'd simply taken care of everything and disappeared.

And Tyler hated that almost as much as being called her friend.

So what are you going to do about it? he asked himself. Unfortunately no answer came immediately to mind.

An hour later, he couldn't take the silence anymore. Funny how he'd used to bask in it all day, and now he couldn't stand not hearing from Tawny.

So he dialed her, only to get her voicemail. Wayne claimed everyone was asleep except for his father, who was in the shower. So they didn't want dinner that night. Wayne said if they did, they'd just order from room service.

So Tyler found himself walking down the beach in his gray slacks and light blue button-up instead of his regular board shorts and T-shirt, dogless, with a grumbling stomach. His mind wasn't much better, and he found his feet taking him away from the eateries dotting the beach and toward Tawny's.

Her bicycle leaned up against the porch, but other than that, the place looked quaint and beachy. Relaxing.

He knocked on the front door and waited, his hands buried in his pockets. A dog barked from somewhere inside the house, and the sound caused Tyler's heart to leap.

A whine followed, and then claws and Tawny's voice

saying something. She opened the door looking a bit flustered. When she saw him, she released Lazy Bones's collar and straightened. "Tyler."

Bones jumped at him, and Tyler laughed as the dog licked his face and ear. "Hey, bud. What have you been doin' over here, huh? Don't tell me Tawny's couch is better than ours." He scrubbed the dog down, glad there was one living thing on the planet that was excited to see him.

"Oh, nothing over here is as nice as what you've got." She leaned in the doorway and chuckled, but it didn't sound entirely happy.

"I've seen your place. It is nice." Why Tyler said that, he wasn't sure. He felt completely out of his element here. All he could hear were his mom's words.

She's beneath you.

All he could feel was the pounding of his heart, telling him he liked Tawny so, so much. He thought maybe it was beating out that he loved her, but he needed to take baby steps.

"What are you doing here?" she asked.

"I called," he said.

"I know."

Tyler didn't know two words could be so sharp and cut so deep. He plowed forward anyway. "I was thinking you might want to go to that string concert?"

Her eyes blazed with fire as bright as the ocean was deep. She loved Hawaiian music, especially the ukuleles and steel guitars.

"Is this a no strings attached evening?"

"No," Tyler said, pushing his dog aside and inching

closer to Tawny. "This is a date." He swallowed, still so unsure of himself. "I mean, I'm dressed up, and you look nice." She always did, but today especially since she'd gone all out to meet his parents. She hadn't changed, and he had the strangest urge to kiss her until her lipstick came off.

"So is that the requirement for a date with you? You have to wear slacks?"

"It's a start," he said, wondering what he'd done wrong. Well, besides tell her he didn't want to be her friend and then doing everything he could to *not* be alone with her so they could talk about it.

"Can the dog come?"

"I don't think so."

Tawny looked between him and Lazy Bones, and Tyler wasn't sure what he'd do if she chose a golden retriever over him.

He squared his shoulders, feeling himself slipping behind that poker mask she'd said she hated, and waited.

SIXTEEN

WATCHING Tyler fade right before her eyes was freaky, and annoying. How easily he covered up everything he was thinking and feeling bothered her, and she couldn't quite pinpoint why.

But the strings concert he'd mentioned was doing a holiday celebration, and Tawny had mentioned it to him as something she thought his family would enjoy. It was Christmasy and islandy, and everything a tourist should like.

"Fine," she said, reaching for Lazy Bones's collar. "You better get back in here, then, dog. We won't have time to eat and get to the concert."

"Oh, so we're eating now too?"

"Of course." She made a big show of checking her phone for the time before tilting it toward him. "It's almost five o'clock."

"Doesn't mean I'm hungry."

She laughed, her head tipping back and the ends of her hair tickling her bare shoulders. The sound silenced when his touch landed on her throat. Just one finger trailed a line from her chin to her collarbone, but it was easily the most sensual touch she'd ever experienced. When he let his hand fall back to his side, she was left cold and wanting.

Their eyes locked, and she couldn't breathe. "I'm going to kiss you now," he said, his voice somewhere stuck in his throat, making him sound husky.

"There's no one around to impress."

"Sure there is." He lowered his mouth to hers, and with that the only point of contact between them, everything about the kiss felt heightened. Every motion, every movement.

He pulled away but didn't back up, didn't go anywhere.

"Tyler," she said, her eyes still closed and her nerves firing on all cylinders.

"Yeah?"

"What's going on here?"

Several beats of silence passed, but she didn't dare open her eyes. He swept one hand down the side of her face, and she leaned into his palm.

"I'm not completely sure," he whispered. "But I think I'm falling in love with you."

Her eyes jerked open then, her heart frantically beating against her ribs, desperate to flee. "What?"

"For real, Tawny," he said earnestly, his blue eyes electric and alive. "Nothing about this feels fake to me. I know it started that way, but I don't...I want...." He exhaled and glanced away. "Tell me I'm not the only one feeling like this." He backed up a step and met her eye again. "Tell me you feel something real for me too."

He swallowed, a big movement in his throat, the only indication that he was nervous at all. Tawny adored the gesture, because it meant he wasn't bottling everything up or hiding behind his perfect poker face.

"All right." His voice pinched along the edges and he fell back another step. "Okay. I see. I...I'm sorry." He turned and went down the steps. "You wanna keep Bones for the night?"

Every cell in her body screamed at her to get him to come back. *Do something. Say something!*

"No," she said.

"All right. I'll take him." He came up the steps to the front porch again.

"No." She stepped in front of him. "No." She shook her head, her emotions spiraling out of control. Tears pricked her eyes, and her voice came out too high when she said, "No, you're not the only one feeling like this."

His eyes searched hers, so full of hope, overflowing with disbelief. "No?"

She shook her head and flung herself into his arms to kiss him again. Just as quickly, she pulled back, her self-pact roaring through her head. She couldn't confess these soft things to him.

"What?" he asked, his lips sliding down her cheek and

landing in the hollow of her neck. She wanted to lean into him and moan her pleasure into the sky.

Instead, she did the opposite and stepped out of his arms.

Shaking her head again, she said, "I think we should stick to the plan." Before she could take that back, and before she could memorize how heartbroken Tyler looked, she spun and went in her house, closing the door behind her decisively.

———

Tawny endured the side looks from Shirley, the muttering under her breath, the way she disagreed about everything Tawny said. It didn't seem possible that a person could argue over personal taste, but Shirley had a knack for doing impossible things.

Tyler came to her defense more than once, and his mom would back off for an hour or two. Once, she went back to the penthouse for a whole afternoon. That had been wonderful, just talking to Tyler's dad and his brother. Gina was always nice, and she did a fair bit of muttering under her breath too. Tawny felt a special bond with her, but she tried not to get too attached, as her and Tyler's break up was just around the corner.

Tyler held her hand if they were in public. Thankfully, they never had to perform a liplock, as she was sure she'd break into tears if she did.

And it was the longest ten days of her life, as kissless as

she was. She slept little and ate less, and agonized over every article of clothing she put on.

She didn't go with Tyler to the airport to send his family back to the mainland but hid on her own private stretch of beach, asking the waves and wind what she should do. She wanted to prolong the relationship with Tyler, which meant she had to end it as soon as possible.

"Where's your boyfriend?"

Tawny almost jumped out of her skin at the sound of the slimy voice. For a fraction of a second, she thought it might be one of the reporters who'd hounded her relentlessly for a couple of weeks.

Then her heart chilled, and she knew she'd be looking into Omar's soulless eyes when she turned around.

"He's not my boyfriend," she snapped. "He's my fiancé."

"Right." He hiked up his pants, and Tawny said, "Don't sit down. Do not sit—" and exhaled as he sat down beside her.

She pulled her knees to her chest and glared at him. "This is a private beach, you know." She'd never been terribly afraid of Omar before, even when she left Cancun in favor of Hawaii. True, he'd been a big reason, but she didn't fear anything from him.

But as she thought about him egging Tyler's house, her arms trembled the slightest bit. "What do you want?" she asked.

"I want you to tell me your engagement to that surfer boy is a mistake."

"It's not a mistake," she said, her heart rapid firing as if to prove her words true. Whatever her relationship with Tyler was, it was *not* a mistake.

"It's certainly not real." He lit a match and held it to the end of his cigar, much to Tawny's dismay. Him starting to smoke meant he intended to stay a while.

Tawny was tired of lying, and she really wanted to just be done with the whole charade. She'd been circling the idea of making her relationship with Tyler real. He'd said his feelings for her were real, but he'd never really said what those feelings were. He didn't need to. She could feel it in every touch, every kiss. Not that there had been any kissing since she'd told him they should stick to the plan.

The plan.

What a stupid plan.

But his parents had left thinking he and Tawny were engaged and would be married as soon as they could decide on a date.

Problem was, she'd started this whole farce to get Omar out of her life, and yet he sat next to her on the sand.

"I'm not going to believe you unless you say it." He puffed out a lungful of smoke, and Tawny might've said anything in that moment to get him to leave. But she held her tongue. She couldn't say it was real, but she didn't have to admit it wasn't either.

Omar chuckled like he'd just heard something really funny, but the sound chilled Tawny to the core. The ocean seemed angry today, like maybe it would decide to be winter for a day or two.

"Well, can you call your dog off?"

"Lazy Bones?"

"No, the fiancé."

"He's not doing anything with you."

"Sure he is."

"Is that why you threw eggs and avocados at his house?"

"I don't know what you're talking about."

"Right." She scoffed. "Just like I don't know what you mean when you say my engagement is fake."

Omar remained mysteriously quiet for way too long before he eventually stood and brushed the sand from his designer suit. "Good-bye, Tawny."

She didn't respond, just let him walk away. It wasn't until much later that she realized he'd said good-bye.

She expected Tyler to call, text, or show up once his family was in the air, flying away from the island. He didn't, and she wasted the hours until bedtime by baking desserts she'd never eat and making new shirts for her yoga classes.

———

The next morning, Tawny taught yoga on the beach, the same as she did almost every morning. The New Year's crowd was big at Sweet Breeze, and apparently everyone was interested in starting their year off right, because her class was easily three times as big as it usually was.

She'd never been happier that she'd cut and tied some new workout shirts. The one she wore today she'd left solid in the back and had cut up the front so her bright yellow bra top showed through.

By the time she finished the class, she wasn't sure she could keep smiling. The crowd dispersed, almost parting like the Red Sea to give her the perfect view of Tyler.

He did not belong on the beach, and she was not the only one staring. He'd exchanged his board shorts for a neatly pressed pair of black slacks, and his faded T-shirt for a bleached white shirt, a blue tie around his neck and falling to the silver belt buckle at his waist.

He looked every bit as rich as he was, and Tawny couldn't swallow, blink, breathe, nothing.

His hair had been cut a couple of inches and he'd slicked it back in that classic way he had, showing the shaved sides, but his face he hadn't shaved.

She packed up her things, taking extra long minutes to do so though she was terribly thirsty and wanted to get off the sand as soon as possible. When she couldn't prolong the moment any longer, she took a deep breath and faced him.

"You look nice," she said, glad her voice came out strong enough.

"I have a meeting," he said coolly, nothing like the man she'd been falling in love with for the past two and a half months.

"Oh, well, good luck." The tension between them could surely be felt up and down the beach, and she was glad she didn't have to fake it. At least then when the news of the break up went public there would be real situations like this to testify of how strained their relationship had become.

He handed her a drink from Two Coconuts, and she

looked at it like she wasn't sure what it was. Such simple gestures like this had her thinking maybe...just maybe....

No, she told herself. Whatever he thought he'd felt while they lied to everyone they knew and loved, he was wrong.

SEVENTEEN

"THANK YOU," Tawny finally said, and Tyler wished things between them could be different. But she'd made herself really clear. She wanted to stick to the plan while he wanted...what did he want?

The engagement to be real. A life with her, the woman he loved. Happiness beyond surfing and throwing a Frisbee and going up to Fisher's penthouse for club meetings.

"Omar wants to meet," he said, losing another debate with himself. He wasn't going to tell her, hoping he could meet with the man and get him out of both of their lives.

"He does?" Her eyes flashed with concern. "Is that why you're all dressed up?"

"I know how to play my part." His voice was barbed and icy, and he hated how petulant it sounded. His unrequited feelings could be so sharp, and he wasn't sure what to do with them most of the time.

"Tyler—"

"Not now," he said, glancing around. "Maybe at dinner tonight? Would you like to break up with me then? We can make it a public spectacle if you'd like." His words dripped with poison, but he couldn't help it. He didn't want to break up with her at all, but he couldn't be with her now that his parents were gone. After he settled everything with Omar, there would be no reason for them to stay together.

Tawny made a squeak of surprise—maybe hurt?—and Tyler nodded to the drink. "That's a new concoction Mo made just for you. He said to stop by and let him know what you think." Tyler turned and took a few steps through the shifting sand. "Text me the details of what you want me to do."

He walked away, desperate for her to call him back. She didn't. He kept breathing. In, then out. He could survive this. He'd done hard things before.

In fact, surviving the holidays was the best Tyler could've hoped for. And he'd done it. He'd put on the best Christmas he knew how to, and he kept everyone happy, and Tawny had played her part perfectly.

Now, if only he didn't feel like his entire life was about to come crashing down around him. He slid into the black car with tinted windows, where his driver had been waiting for the past thirty minutes while Tyler watched Tawny finish teaching her class before he could talk to her.

Simply seeing her was torture, and he wondered how he could survive living only a half a mile from her and not be hers.

"I'm ready," he said to his driver, and Georgia got the car moving. Tyler stared out the window as they drove down the main streets and away from the beach. Hawaii had great hills covered in lush vegetation, with waterfalls and lava cliffs.

Omar had asked to meet with him in the mansion where he'd been staying since October. Tyler had alerted Fisher, Jasper, and Marshall, and all three of them were currently stationed at Jasper's estate, which was just up the road.

Georgia put in the gate code Tyler had gotten from Omar and they went up the hill to the sprawling house.

"Thirty minutes," Tyler told her. "If I don't come out in thirty minutes, call this number." He handed her a slip of paper with Jasper's phone number on it and steeled his nerves. He had a feeling he'd need his wits and all of his poker skills to get through this meeting.

The walk toward the front door seemed to take forever, and someone opened it before he even had to knock. "This way," the man said, and Tyler took one more breath before entering the lion's den.

The house smelled falsely of lemons, like someone had burned a candle or sprayed something to cover up the scent of leftover cigar smoke. Tyler tried to take in as many details as possible, but the man led him toward the left and into a library, his final destination.

Omar was already there, and he said, "Oh, he's here," as Tyler entered.

Three more men turned, each of them holding a tumbler of amber liquid Tyler assumed was whiskey.

He'd drunk his fair share of the alcohol while on the poker circuit, but he hadn't had a drop since Holly had told him she was pregnant. He'd regretted too much while he was drinking, and he didn't want to be that man again.

Omar took a long draw on his cigar, but he did not stand. Tyler remained near the door, sizing up the four men in the room. They were all bigger than him, and the only chance of him surviving this if something went south was sheer time.

Thirty minutes. He had to keep Omar talking for that long, or get the meeting over with quick.

"You got me here," Tyler said. "What do you want?"

No one moved, and Omar regarded him with malice in those dark eyes. He finally flicked two fingers, setting the men into motion. "Come, sit."

Tyler smoothed down his tie and did as instructed.

"It has come to my knowledge that your engagement with Tawny Loveless is fake," Omar said.

"That's not true," Tyler said, maybe a bit too fast and a bit too defensively.

Omar switched his gaze from Tyler to one of his men, and he pressed a button. A recording played with Omar's voice and then Tawny's, where she didn't confirm or deny that the engagement was fake.

Until she said, "Just like I don't know what you mean when you say my engagement is fake," in an ultra-sarcastic voice. She might as well have put it on the Internet.

"I'm willing to destroy the tape...for the right price."

Tyler blinked at him, sure he'd heard wrong. "You're blackmailing me?"

Omar shrugged. "Think of it as paying for a service. My service of silence."

Tyler stood and walked away. "Not going to happen. I'll see myself out."

"I will put this up everywhere. Everyone will know you and Tawny have been lying for months."

Tyler paused with his hand on the doorknob. He turned back to Omar and his goons. "I don't care what you do with that tape. It means nothing. She didn't say anything." He took one step back toward Omar. "So you do what you want with it."

Omar stood then, his eyes flickering dangerously. "I did not believe it, but I can see it's true."

"What?" Tyler snapped, his patience wearing very thin.

"You're in love with her."

"I am not."

Omar stalked closer, a tiger after its prey. "Please, don't insult me. I too have been in love with the beautiful Tawny Loveless. I know what it looks like." He stopped only a few feet from Tyler, who felt rooted to the spot. "And you're in love with her."

"So what if I am?" Tyler sincerely hoped this conversation wasn't being recorded, but he couldn't do anything about it if it was.

A look of pity came across Omar's face. "I'm going back to Mexico tomorrow."

"That's great," Tyler said without inflection in his tone. "Take your tape with you, and leave Tawny alone." That was all he really wanted. He turned and opened the door, somewhat surprised Omar let him go so easily.

Still, a slip of trepidation passed over his shoulders as he walked away, exposing his back to the man.

He'd just reached the front door, when Omar called his name. Tyler twisted back, not committing fully to facing him.

"For what it's worth, I think she's in love with you too," he said.

"If you love her—if you've ever loved her—you won't release that tape," Tyler said, trying one last tactic. He didn't wait for Omar to answer. He got out of there, not daring to hope that anything Omar had said could be true.

———

True to his word, Omar returned to Mexico the following day. Tyler couldn't get Tawny on the phone to schedule a time for them to break up. After the third day, he quit trying. Maybe she assumed that would just be enough, and he'd be able to tell his family that the wedding was off.

But he didn't, not even Wayne, like maybe if his mother still thought he and Tawny were engaged that they were.

A week into January, Tyler came in from surfing to find Lazy Bones had betrayed him again. This time the golden retriever sat next to Jason Barnes, the reporter from Aces High. Tyler eyed him warily and wiped the water from his hair.

"I want the exclusive," Jason said. "For Aces High, to

come out forty-eight hours before any other news outlet gets wind of the story."

"I have no idea what you're talking about."

Jason extended his hand toward Tyler, and he took a micro SD card from him. "What's this?"

"Your confession that the engagement was fake. Omar Velasquez gave it to me."

"He gave it to you?" Tyler wanted to squeeze the tiny plastic rectangle until it cracked in half. "Or you bought it from him?"

"Does it matter?"

Tyler locked eyes with Jason. "It does to me."

"Aces High bought it."

Disgust roared through Tyler, but he also wondered if Omar somehow needed money...he shook his head. Not his problem. Omar had left the island and Tyler hoped he wouldn't come back.

"It's not my only copy," Jason added. "So you don't need to be real careful with it."

"Great." Tyler dropped it in the sand and kicked it away from him before dropping to the ground on the other side of Lazy Bones. He stared at the waves he'd just been in, the peace he stole from them each morning already gone.

"I get to tell my family first." He cut Jason a look out of the corner of his eye. "Then you can have your exclusive."

A grin touched the other man's lips for a fraction of a second. "And I'll want to talk to Tawny."

"Yeah, well, get in line." Tyler didn't mean for so much frustration to coat the syllables.

"Oh, so there's actual trouble in paradise?"

"No paradise to begin with," Tyler said. "Didn't you listen to the tape? It was fake."

Jason remained quiet for a moment, and then he said, "Yeah, what I saw wasn't fake."

The schoolboy in Tyler wanted to beg Jason to tell Tawny that, but he clamped his jaw shut and said nothing.

"So how much time do you need?" Jason asked.

"I can tell my family today."

"Great." He stood and patted Lazy Bones, who wore that ridiculous doggie smile that prevented Tyler from staying mad at him for very long. "Then let's interview this afternoon, and I'll get in touch with Tawny. I can have something ready in a few days."

Tyler nodded, glad when Jason left him sitting there in his wetsuit, and jealous that the man would get to talk to Tawny and he wouldn't.

———

Later that day, after the interview was complete, he sat in the hammock and pushed himself back and forth. It felt good to tell the truth for once, and he hoped Jason would take it and do something good with it.

He felt scattered, lost, scared, alone. He needed to call Tawny. Her voice would soothe him. For some reason, he'd imagined them going through this break up together. That they'd reassure each other that they were doing the right thing, that neither of them had gotten hurt, that his family would forgive him.

But none of that felt true as her line rang and rang and rang.

He didn't feel like breaking up was the right thing. He had definitely been hurt—his chest felt like someone had carved his heart out and left a huge hole behind. And he wasn't entirely sure his mother would speak to him again once he told her the truth.

He called Tawny, telling himself it was to warn her about the tape, Jason's interview, all of it.

"Jason's got proof the engagement was fake," Tyler said to Tawny's voicemail. "I'm calling my parents as soon as I hang up here." He paused, his mind going in ten different directions. "Please call me back when you get this so I know you've gotten it."

He paced for another ten minutes, psyching himself up to call his mom. When he finally got his fingers to tap the right buttons, his whole body was tight.

"Tyler, dear, how are you?"

"You know what, Mom? I've been better." He exhaled and reminded himself that he was an adult, had plenty of money, and that his mother lived thousands of miles away.

"Oh? What's going on?"

"Tawny and I broke up," he said. "The engagement is off. And actually, funny story, it was all sort of a ruse to begin with...."

EIGHTEEN

WEATHERING storms had never really been Tawny's strong suit. She quit jobs, ran from resorts, or disappeared inside her house for days on end.

Tyler kept trying to talk to her, and she couldn't fathom why. So she ignored his call and slid another pan of brownies in the oven. It would join the cookies, lemon bars, and cakes she'd made over the past week. Her freezer was quite full, but she'd have treats for the next six months for the Women's Beach Club. And she was going to need them—the desserts and the women in the club.

She curled into the couch, the loss of Lazy Bones beside her somewhat heartbreaking too. Her mind and her heart seemed constantly at war, and they also seemed to enjoy playing tricks on the other.

The timer went off on the brownies, and she startled, realizing she'd lost fifty minutes of her life to staring. The doorbell pealed at the same time, and she stood, unsure of which to get first.

Since she was steps from the door, she went that way and opened it. "I have a timer going off. Give me two—" Everything in her from her pulse to her voice froze.

Tyler stood on the front porch as windswept and handsome as ever. "I'll wait," he said, his voice smooth as velvet and rich as chocolate.

Tawny couldn't move, couldn't think, couldn't speak.

"I'll get it." He eased past her, very careful not to touch her, she noted. So maybe her mind worked when it wanted to. The incessant beeping stopped a moment later, followed by a clang and a scrape as he pulled the brownies from the oven.

That launched her feet into motion, and she hurried down the foyer and into the kitchen.

"What's going on here?" he asked, surveying the assorted baked goods on the counter. He couldn't seem to settle on the chocolate chip cookies or the carrot cake or the pumpkin roll. And he certainly wasn't looking at her.

"Just a little baking." She cleared her throat, somewhat frustrated he affected her so strongly. She wondered how long she'd have to deal with the accelerated pulse every time she saw him, the wishful longing when she thought about him at night, the tears that threatened to spill down her cheeks at the drop of a hat. Or in this case, the simple act of removing her brownies from the oven for her.

"Did you get my message?"

"Which one?"

That brought his eyes to hers, and they were bright, and bold, and furious. "The one I left an hour ago."

"No, I haven't had time to check." She wasn't even entirely sure where her phone was.

"Well, Jason knows the engagement was fake." Tyler leaned against the counter and folded his arms, softening into the surfer boy she loved so much. "Omar had a confession on tape or something, and Aces High bought it. I just did an exclusive interview with him, and he wants to meet with you too."

He'd said a lot, and Tawny's body had reacted in pieces. Cold from knowing the truth was out there. Hot from thinking the world would know it very soon. Scared that she'd never be able to give as good of an interview as Tyler—and how stupid was that? She wasn't inferior to him; he'd never made her feel that way. And yet she felt that way now.

"Why?" she asked. "Why give him anything?"

Tyler shrugged. "I like the guy. If the story's going to come out anyway, he might as well get the glory."

How he was so utterly nonplussed about this boggled her mind. "Don't you care about the story getting out?"

"Not really." He brought his gaze back to her and this time it raged from hot to cold and back again. "We're basically over anyway, right? I mean, you won't even call me back. Send a text." He nudged a paper plate laden with cookies. "Bring me a treat."

She shook her head, but she didn't know how to follow it up with words.

"No?" he asked, always able to vocalize things when

she couldn't. Or at least partial things. "No what, Tawny?"

No, we're not over.

Yes, I'll bring you cookies.

She turned away from him and let her eyes roam the back yard and beach beyond the window. "I'm sorry I messed your life up," she said. "That was never my intent."

The oven clicked a reminder that it was still on in the ensuing silence. He ground this throat and said, "I think I've made it quite clear you haven't messed my life up."

That insane hope floated through her, and she hugged herself. "I feel messed up," she said. "I've done everything backward, and I don't know how to fix it."

He stepped closer to her, the heat from his body in the already warm kitchen like a balm to her soul. She wanted to lean into him, but she stopped herself.

"What do you mean you've done everything backward?"

She gave a mirthless laugh. "Since I've had such a rough time in the dating pool lately, I decided to do everything the opposite of what I'd normally do." She faced him, finally feeling strong enough to tell him something real. "So if I wanted to hold your hand, I didn't. If I wanted to tell you something intimate, I held back. If I wanted to kiss you, I waited for you to kiss me first."

Her breath came quickly now as he searched her face, a measure of horror on his.

"So…you're saying not only was this relationship fake, you were fake with me too? This whole time?"

Tawny wanted to erase the childlike hurt from his

voice, but it reverberated through her ears, her brain, her skull as if someone had hit a gong.

She felt twisted up and put together wrong. "I guess so," she said. "I guess it was an experiment that didn't work out." She remembered Sasha warning her to just be herself. But that had never worked for Tawny.

This didn't work either, her mind screamed.

An angry, explosive sound burst from his mouth. "I gave Jason your number." He walked away, his footsteps strong and sure and the door slamming closed behind him the very final punctuation mark to their break up.

———

Three days later, Tawny sat on the beach, almost in the exact same spot as she had when Omar had visited her for the last time. Deep down, she knew she wouldn't see him again. He'd taped their conversation and she hadn't known it.

Betrayal tasted bitter, but she swallowed it down. *Doesn't matter*, she thought. The truth about her and Tyler was bound to come out. This way would just be a little more public. It didn't matter, not for her. She wasn't the billionaire poker celebrity with a reputation to protect.

"Is this patch of sand taken?"

She glanced up at Jason and waved down the beach. "It's all yours."

He wasn't wearing beach-appropriate attire, but he flopped to the sand like he really wanted grains in the pleats of his slacks. "I'm glad you finally called me back."

She said nothing, the idea that had been tickling her mind for days now practically shouting at her. "When will the article be published?" she asked to try to drown out the voice.

"Not until the next issue—February tenth."

"That's almost a month." Living without Tyler in her life for another month sounded impossible. Couldn't be done. Her heart rammed her ribcage, demanding a special edition be printed before then.

"Yep. Gotta keep this under wraps for a while longer." He pulled out a recorder. "So I just want to hear how things went from your perspective."

She met his eye. "How things went?"

"Yeah, how the relationship started, why the fake engagement, what you're going to do now."

She glared at the device he held on his knee. "And you could use anything I say?"

"Well, that's kind of the deal." He pulled a folder from his briefcase. "All the legal documents are in here. You'll have to sign them for me to use something you say."

She took the folder but didn't open it. "What if I asked you to spin the article in a certain way?"

"What do you mean?"

"Do you think Tyler will read the article?"

Jason blinked, the surprise evident in his beat of silence. "I honestly have no idea."

"Can you make sure he reads it?"

"He's isolated himself from the poker community. I doubt he reads anything related to the industry anymore."

"Can you send him a copy? Highly suggest he read it?"

Jason cocked his head, that flop of dark hair shifting with the movement and the breeze. "Why?"

Tawny swallowed, the idea going to burst from her despite her attempt to hold it back. "Because I fell in love with him, and I've made a lot of mistakes, and I want to get him back."

Jason exhaled and looked out toward the water, the end of his sigh sounding like a hiss. "So you want me to put something in there about all of that. Sort of your apology and that you love him, *which* I'm assuming you haven't told him."

"Yeah, that's about it. And when he sees it...." She shrugged, remembering the angry way he'd marched away from her. "Maybe he'll accept my apology and come back."

"Are you sure this is the best idea?" Jason asked. "Tyler's a pretty private guy from what I've gathered."

"It's the only idea I have," she said. Esther and Stacey had asked a lot of questions about Tawny's idea too, but she couldn't meet with her Beach Club every day and air her doubts and worries. She had to make some decisions on her own.

"All right," he said. "I'll do what I can. I have a job to do too."

"Of course."

He shook the recorder slightly. "Okay, so if you'll just start at the beginning...."

Tawny took a deep breath. "The first time I met Tyler, he'd thrown his dog's Frisbee near my beach yoga class...."

NINETEEN

TAWNY FOLLOWED Tyler in his dreams, into the waves in the morning, everywhere. He couldn't get away from thoughts of her, almost like they were specters determined to haunt him forever.

When she'd told him that she'd done everything backward, he'd never felt so duped. Even when he'd lost in the last round of a qualifying tournament to a guy who'd deliberately concealed a card for the entire game.

Tyler knew what it felt like to lose, and to win, and to be taken advantage of. He knew the taste of betrayal, and heartache, and none of it was something he wanted to repeat again.

Hadn't he left all of that behind when he'd come to Hawaii?

He'd tried.

But this trickery felt more personal. Stronger, and

harder, and more lethal than anything he'd ever experienced before.

He'd fallen in love with a woman pretending to be someone else. He didn't know Tawny Loveless at all—and yet it hurt with a pain so deep down in his gut that Tyler couldn't even make it through breakfast without thinking about calling her.

Instead, he pulled up their text string and read through it. He had the time, and he never deleted anything from his phone. In the end, he always returned to the angry, agitated state he existed in now.

He swung in the hammock, only the breeze and Bones for company, when voices reached his ears. He perked up, the timbre familiar. Sure enough, Fisher, Marshall, and Jasper rounded the corner of his house, all of them wearing slacks and button-up shirts, closed at the throat with ties.

"I knew you'd be back here," Fisher said. He didn't smile, and Tyler relaxed back into the hammock again.

"It isn't rocket science," he said.

"You've missed our last two meetings." Jasper came all the way to the end of the hammock and folded his arms.

"Not really dealing with business right now," Tyler said. He had an appointment with his account managers next week, and he hadn't quite gotten up the nerve to cancel it yet. But he could avoid the Nine-0 club easily, so he had.

"Oh, he's in bad shape," Marshall said.

"I'm fine," Tyler said.

"What happened that was so bad?" Fisher sat at the

picnic table a few feet away and rolled up his shirtsleeves.

Tyler didn't need to get into all the details. "I feel like I barely know her." That was the root of the problem. Oh, and the fact that he'd practically told her he loved her, and she'd thrown it back in his face with *let's stick to the plan.*

He'd had no idea her plans were to be fake to the outside world *and* with him.

"So get to know her again," Marshall said.

"It's not that easy." Tyler tossed him a dark look.

"If it's any consolation, she looks miserable too." Fisher lifted one shoulder in a shrug. "She still shows up to work, but she's different."

Tyler scoffed. "Yeah, she's probably back to acting like herself." That would be different from the woman he thought he knew, the woman he thought he'd fallen in love with. "I just feel stupid, you know? Like, I can *read people.* I used to do it for a living. And I couldn't tell she was lying to me while we were lying to everyone else." Frustration built inside him, but he pushed out his breath violently, hoping some of the negative emotion would go with it.

"Maybe you're just rusty," Marshall said.

"Or maybe…." Jasper looked at the other men. "Maybe you saw the real her." He lifted one eyebrow and cocked his head. "Maybe she just thought she wasn't being her true self."

"What does that even mean?" Tyler asked.

"Why do you think you don't know her?" Jasper countered.

"She said she'd done everything backward with me,

because all of her previous relationships hadn't worked out. Said it was an *experiment* that didn't work out."

Jasper considered what he'd said. "Well, that doesn't mean *she* was different. Just what she chose to do."

"It's the same thing, Jasper."

"I don't think so."

"We'll agree to disagree." Tyler was done with this conversation. "Is there something you guys needed? I'm busy here."

"Tyler—" Fisher started, but he stopped when Tyler glared at him. He stood. "All right. Let's leave him alone. He knows where to find us."

"And where to find Tawny," Jasper added as he walked away. "I hope he doesn't let her get away. Although, if he does, maybe I'll ask her out." He kept talking, but a roar of jealous rage blanketed Tyler's ears in white noise.

No way *anyone* else could go out with Tawny. Kiss Tawny.

He shook his head. She wasn't his anymore. In fact, she never had been.

Lazy Bones whined from his spot underneath Tyler, and he let his hand fall down onto the dog's side. "I know, bud. I miss her too."

So much his heart barely knew how to beat anymore.

———

A week passed, and then two, and Tyler still hadn't figured out a way back to the life he'd had before the hospital gala. He went through the motions of meeting with his account managers, and eating, and even attending one Nine-0 meeting. He barely heard two words, but he'd gotten dressed and he'd left the house.

With Valentine's Day right around the corner, he was considering a trip off the island. He had plenty of time and money, and he thought about packing a bag and showing up at the airport and asking for a ticket on the next plane that was taking off. Whatever he didn't have, he could buy when he landed.

One day, while he threw the Frisbee for Bones, his phone rang. A rush of adrenaline made his heart ba-bump with the hope that it could be Tawny. But it was Fisher, and that was actually good, because then Tyler could actually answer the call.

"Yeah," he said. "What's up, Fisher?"

"Have you gotten the mail yet today?"

"My mail?" Tyler turned back toward his house, which sat down the beach a bit. "I'm out with Bones. I don't know if it's come."

"You need to check it."

"Why?" While he normally enjoyed leafing through the mail—it was at least something that took up fifteen minutes of his miserable existence—no one ever sent him anything good.

"You just do."

Tyler couldn't judge Fisher's mood by his tone of voice. "What do I need to know?" He picked up the Frisbee Bones had just dropped at his feet, and instead of throwing it out into the water, this time, he tossed it back toward his house.

As Bones tore after it, Tyler walked that way, forcing the dog back to the house.

"Nothing," Fisher said. "You just really need to get your mail."

"Fine. Is that all?"

Fisher laughed. "Yes, that's all."

"Great." Tyler hung up and kept throwing the Frisbee back toward the house until he and Bones made it to the yard. He made sure the dog had plenty of cold water, which he lapped up enthusiastically, and then Tyler went around the house to the front to collect the mail.

He had quite the stack of useless envelopes, solicitations for credit cards, a couple of flyers for landscapers on the island, a coupon book, and a magazine.

He didn't subscribe to magazines.

He flipped it over and found Aces High staring back at him. This issue had a well-dressed man on the cover, the current high-money winner on the circuit. Tyler remembered when he'd been on the cover of dozens of poker-related magazines, and he dropped the pile of mail.

The story was out.

No wonder Fisher had called. Tyler dialed him back, not sure if he was angry, irritated, or just plain old tired.

"You wanted me to see the Aces High magazine?"

"Yeah, you got it?"

Tyler stared at it on the ground. "I got it."

"Are you going to read it?"

He scoffed. "No. Why would I do that?"

"It's good."

"*You* read it? Since when do you subscribe to Aces

High?"

"The story's online."

"Great." Tyler looked heavenward, really needing some divine intervention to make it through the next several hours. He suspected his phone would blow up with calls and texts from the friends he'd left behind or his brother, though Wayne and the rest of his family already knew about the fake engagement.

"Read it," Fisher said. "It's good."

"I don't need proof of Jason's great journalism." He toed the offending magazine on the ground. "I don't even know how I got one."

"I'm sure Jason sent it to you."

He could've, but Tyler wasn't so sure, especially if the article was online. "I have to go," Tyler said.

"Oh yeah? Pressing deadline approaching?" Fisher laughed and ended the call. Tyler envied his carefree laughter. He felt like he may never laugh again.

He wasn't the type of person to leave a pile of mail on the front lawn, so he scooped it up, magazine and all, and went inside.

The magazine mocked him from where he put it on the counter. He did his best to ignore it as he pulled a water bottle from the fridge and then went to let Lazy Bones in from the back yard.

Aces High felt like it had the gravitational pull of the sun, and he kept rotating back to it. He finally picked it up and leafed through the first few pages, just to see what articles there were.

"Stupid," he said, adding a scoff and tossing the magazine back to the counter.

But he knew he'd read it eventually, and he just wanted to get it over with. Stop torturing himself. His phone hadn't so much as beeped yet, and maybe Wayne was having an exceptionally busy afternoon behind his pod of computer screens.

He grabbed the magazine and went to his hammock, the safest place to read about his fake engagement to a woman that had anything but false feelings flowing through him.

The article wasn't hard to find; it wasn't buried near the back, with only half a page for the headline and no pictures.

Oh, no. Jason had made the most of his exclusive, and the title sang from the page in bright, bold, capital red letters.

THE POKER PRINCE'S ROYAL FLUSH

Tyler appreciated the wit, and he enjoyed Jason's easy, conversational style of writing. He had all the facts right, and a couple of quotes from Tyler on why he'd done it.

"I just wanted to help her out. She seemed so panicked when that other guy came up to us, and I made a mistake."

He *had* made a mistake. He shouldn't have agreed to much of anything, let alone an engagement that went on for almost three months. After all, that gala was supposed to be no strings attached.

He went back to the article, and the perspective shifted to Tawny. Jason said she corroborated Tyler's story and genuinely seemed apologetic that they'd lied to their friends and family.

The article only had a few more inches in it when Jason wrote, *And now Tawny wants to finish the story in her own words.*

"I just want everyone out there reading this to know how wonderful Tyler is. He stepped up when someone else wouldn't have."

Tyler felt like someone had dropped a piano on his chest, but he forced himself to keep reading.

I want his family to know that I didn't mean to hurt them.

"I want Tyler to know that I fell in love with him months ago, and I'd do almost anything to make things right with him. He probably won't read this, because he's probably surfing or throwing a Frisbee to his dog.

But I don't want the world to think I was after his money. I wasn't. I was after his heart, and I didn't realize how much I loved him until I realized I'd already given him mine."

Tyler blinked, sure he'd read the quotes wrong. He went back, and the words were the same. Jason finished the article with, *There you have it, poker fans. The Prince isn't coming back any time soon, and maybe, just maybe, if he plays his cards right, he and Tawny will end up with a real engagement. It's this reporter's opinion, having spent time with them together, and both of them apart, that they genuinely love each other. And if the world needs more of anything, it's love.*

The magazine fell to Tyler's chest, and he lay in the hammock for a moment, utterly stunned. Then he launched himself out of the hammock, the magazine clutched in his fist, hoping he could do exactly what Jason had said and play his cards right.

TWENTY

TAWNY SMEARED the last of the mint frosting over the pan of brownies, intending to take them to her yoga class the following morning. It was a few days before Valentine's Day and Sweet Breeze was full of sickeningly sweet couples. Couples celebrating. Couples on anniversary trips. Couples, couples, couples.

Tawny was taking two days off, something she hardly ever did. She wouldn't see her regulars until she came back after Valentine's Day, so she wanted to give them a treat before she left.

She was even leaving the island for the duration of her time off. The smaller island of Maui had beautiful hikes and waterfalls, and she could do those alone without anyone asking her why she didn't have a date.

Someone knocked on the door, startling her. Because it was more like pounding than anything else.

"Tawny!" a man called, and for one horrible moment,

she thought Omar had returned to the island to claim her as his.

She dropped the off-set spatula and then snatched it back up again as she crept to the corner and peered down the hall to the front door.

It opened, and he said, "Tawny?" again.

She stepped out and planted her feet, lifting the frosting-covered utensil in front of her like it could do any damage to anyone.

Tyler came through the door, gripping something in one hand. He saw her standing there and froze.

She couldn't move either, and her heart wailed inside her chest. "It's February tenth," she whispered, her mouth barley moving. And he'd obviously gotten the magazine. Jason had sent her the article a couple of days ago, saying he couldn't change anything at that point but that he thought he'd done a decent job doing what she'd asked.

More than decent, she'd texted back. All she'd been able to do was hope and pray that Tyler would read it and somehow find a way to forgive her.

He lifted the rolled up magazine. "Is this true?"

"Every word."

"You told Jason all of this?"

"Right to his recorder." And now the whole world knew too. Well, those who cared about poker, which admittedly, wasn't that many people.

His gaze burned her from fifteen feet away. "What are you going to do with that?" He nodded to the spatula.

Tawny lowered it and then quickly took a few steps into the kitchen and dropped it back to the counter before returning to him. He'd come. He'd read the article and come to see her.

Her turn to be brave.

"I'm in love with you," she said, taking slow, measured steps toward him. "I didn't believe you when you said similar things, because I was sort of in this weird place inside my own head, and doing all kinds of strange things, and...yeah." She sucked in a breath and told herself not to keep babbling.

He just stared at her, and it was a horrible feeling to say she loved him and not have him say it back.

Finally, he tossed the magazine onto her couch and took four strong steps toward her. "I love you, Tawny," he said before he reached for her. She expected his touch to be rough, but it was gentle, soft as he cupped her face and gazed into her eyes. "You have my heart too."

When he kissed her, the joy and heat exploded through her until she saw stars. Or maybe they were hearts. Spades. Whatever. She was in love with the man kissing her, and she wasn't going to hide it anymore.

———

"Bones," Tyler called up the path, and the golden retriever stalled. He didn't turn and look back, but he waited, his tongue hanging out of his mouth until Tawny and Tyler caught up to him.

"I'll put you on the leash if I have to," Tyler threatened, but Tawny knew he'd do no such thing. Bones gave him a baleful look and started walking again as if to say, *Well, hurry up then. You humans walk so slow.*

But Tawny wasn't in any hurry. The path through this tropical paradise seemed too beautiful to be true, and the rushing sounds of water falling over cliffs was loud in her ears, which meant they were almost there.

With this second day of their quick vacation to Maui almost over, Tawny wanted to prolong every moment until she had to return to Getaway Bay and her real life.

Though, now that Tyler was back in her daily routine, things had started to look up considerably.

They climbed a bit farther, Bones staying a nose ahead of Tyler, and rounded a curve. The waterfall field spread before them, the most glorious thing Tawny had ever seen. She pulled in a breath and said, "Isn't it the most beautiful thing you've ever seen?"

"No." Tyler pulled her close and kissed her cheek. "That would be you."

She grinned and warmed at his words, snuggling deeper into his side.

"Should we eat?" he asked, slipping his pack off one shoulder. He'd told her he'd take care of all the details of food, activities, lodging. And he had. If it were possible, Tawny had fallen deeper in love with him in the past two days.

They'd had plenty to talk about too, and in the end, he'd said, "I felt like I didn't know you at all once you'd told me you were doing things backward. But I see now that you can't help being you."

"And that's okay?"

"Tawny." He'd taken both of her hands in his. "You're all I want. You're exactly who I need in my life. You're everything I didn't even know I wanted."

And Tawny had believed him. She ate to the chorus of falling water, Tyler lost in his own world. Truth be told, Tawny was too.

The sun started to set, and that got her to get moving. "Hey, so we should head back. It'll be dark before we come off the trail if we don't."

"Yeah, sure." But he didn't get up. He took his time packing up his trash and stuffing it in his pack. She wandered over to the edge of the path with Bones and watched the water pound down into the pool below.

"I just have something I want to talk to you about before we go."

Tawny turned back to him to find him down on both knees, a diamond ring pinched between two fingers.

"I sort of really liked being your fiancé," he said. "And I love you with all my heart. I'm wondering if you'd like to wear this ring again, this time for real."

"For real?" she echoed, sure they'd had the shortest time from first date to engagement in the history of the earth. Both times.

"For real," he confirmed. "You'd make me the happiest man in Hawaii if you'd be my wife."

"Do we have to set a date right away?"

His eyes twinkled. "Of course not."

"Will there be strings attached?"

"Lots and lots of them."

Tawny stepped closer and looked at the ring. "This is a different ring."

"Yeah, you still have the other one." He grinned at her. "Plus, Jasper said this one's way better for a legit engagement ring."

"So he sold us a lemon last time?"

"I actually didn't buy that ring, so I'm gonna need it back."

Tawny tipped her head back and laughed. She sobered and bent down to look him straight in the eye. "I would love to be your wife. I love you, and I hope there are so many strings, we get tangled up together for a long time."

He slid the ring on her finger, and it felt right. Not too heavy, like last time.

She kissed him, pure delight and happiness to be finally kissing her fiancé surging through her.

———

Read on for a sneak peek at **STRAW AND DIAMONDS,** **the next book in the Getaway Bay Resort series.**

SNEAK PEEK! STRAW AND DIAMONDS CHAPTER ONE

SASHA REDDING ARRIVED last to the beach, the group of women before her already laughing about something. Of course they had things to giggle over. Boyfriends. Dates that evening. Diamond rings.

She dropped her beach chair to the sand with a little too much force. Fine, maybe she threw it. No matter what, sand sprayed out and hit Esther on the right and Tawny on the left. Esther glanced up at her, her ultra-blonde hair practically white in the sunshine.

Tawny kept on talking as if she hadn't even noticed Sasha's arrival. And wasn't that the epitome of Sasha's life? She sighed as she sprayed sunscreen on her bare arms and shoulders and settled into her chair.

Tawny had recently broken up with her boyfriend. Or her fake fiancé. The fake fiancé that she'd fallen in love with. But even though they weren't speaking at the moment, Sasha knew they'd get back together. It was only a matter of time before the article in that poker magazine came out and Tyler—the fake fiancé/boyfriend—would come around and forgive her.

Sasha didn't have a fiancé, real or otherwise. Nor a boyfriend. Nor anyone interested in becoming her boyfriend or fiancé. It was a problem that, until very recently, all the women in the Beach Club had been dealing with.

But one by one, love had claimed them all. Okay, just three of them, but it felt like all of them to Sasha, as the other ladies were a bit older and adamant they didn't want another boyfriend or husband.

Sasha secretly did though, and when Tawny finally finished talking, Esther turned her and asked, "Everything okay?"

No, everything was no okay. Sasha didn't want to talk about it, but at the same time, she didn't have anyone else to tell. And wasn't that why she came to these little get-togethers? It wasn't to see the glinting diamonds, that was for sure.

"I'm taking a second job," she said. "Starts tomorrow." She stared out across the water, the winter sunlight still bright enough to hurt her eyes as it reflected off the bay.

"Things are that bad?" Esther leaned forward and peered at Sasha, obviously trying to get her to face her.

"Yes." Sasha didn't want to admit that she used money for her drink stand, The Straw, that she should've used to pay her electric bill. But if she didn't have The Straw, she wouldn't have any income. So she was a bit behind right now. She'd get caught up as soon as she started getting paid from this new job.

"What are you doing?" Tawny asked. "For the new job, I mean."

"I'm cleaning some rich guy's house," she said, the words like poison on her tongue. She'd definitely had enough of wealthy men, that was for sure. Stacey, Esther, and Tawny didn't seem to mind them, but Sasha preferred to meet a simple fisherman, or maybe a busboy. They, at least, wouldn't give her unsolicited advice about how she should run her business.

"Who?" Tawny asked, and Stacey and Esther looked more than interested too. Winnie, another Hawaiian woman in their group, kept her face placidly turned toward the sun as if she wasn't listening to the conversation.

"I don't know," Sasha said. "Jasper something."

"Jasper Rosequist?" Tawny practically screeched the name, which finally got Sasha to look at her.

"Yeah. Do you know him?"

"He's friends with Tyler."

"And Fisher," Stacey said.

"And Marshall." Esther's right eyebrow cocked, and a small smile joined the party.

"So what?" Sasha asked. "I'm not going to fall in love with him." They all knew about Newton and what he'd done to her stand, her life, her heart. No, she didn't need another man with money to come shred everything she'd had to rebuild. Not again.

"So here's an idea," Esther said. "Why not just give him

a try?"

"How about we don't?" Sasha glared at her friend.

Tawny nodded, more enthusiastically than the situation warranted. "You might like him."

"I don't care. Number one, he's my boss."

"And number two?" Stacey asked.

"I won't even see him. He made it very clear he works all night and sleeps during the day. I'm supposed to show up at six AM." She groaned just thinking about being up that early. "Work for a few hours—pretty quietly too—and slip out so I don't disturb him." She made air quotes around the last two words. "He's high maintenance already." The complete opposite of a busboy.

"So then we'll bet," Esther said simply.

Sasha growled, but the other girls didn't care. In fact, Winnie said, "I'll put in fifty bucks if she'll ask him out."

"I'll match that," Esther said.

"I'll double it," Stacey added.

"I'm poor," Tawny said. "But I'll put in twenty if he says yes."

Sasha started shaking her head about the time Stacey had spoken, but the thought of two hundred and twenty dollars had her reconsidering. That could pay for a lot of cups…or get her electricity back on.

"I'm not asking him out," she said, though the idea was still tickling the back of her mind.

"Well, if you do." Esther shrugged.

"There should be a time limit," Stacey said. "Within the first week or something."

"Two weeks," Tawny said. "Maybe she won't even see

him in the first week. You know?"

"All right." Esther beamed as brightly as the sun. "Sasha has to ask out Jasper within two weeks, starting tomorrow, for a grand prize pot of two hundred and twenty dollars."

"*If* he says yes," Tawny amended. "I'm only paying if he says yes." She grinned at Sasha, who couldn't quite return the gesture. "Which I'm sure he will, because you're gorgeous."

"Fine." Esther looked from Tawny to Sasha. "Two-twenty if he says yes. Two hundred if she asks him, no matter what he says. We're all in agreement?"

Everyone agreed, except Sasha, who rolled her eyes and said, "I hate you guys," before facing the bay again and wondering if she really could make an easy two hundred dollars with a simple question.

———

The following morning, Sasha certainly didn't feel gorgeous. She wore her strawberry blonde hair in a high ponytail and tight-fitting athleisure wear that she could get sweaty in and not care.

Jasper had given her the code to the lock on the front door, and she tapped it in to the chorus of beeps. Something clicked and she pushed open the double-tall entrance. This place was ridiculous, and she waffled again on whether she'd even be able to look a man like Jasper Rosequist in the eye.

She was five minutes early, but he wasn't paying her by

the hour. He'd said over the phone that he'd leave her a list on a table in the foyer each day, and she'd get paid five hundred dollars every Friday if she completed the jobs. Simple. Easy. Way more money than simple, easy house-cleaning required. But she wasn't complaining about the salary.

The table sat ten feet from her, a gorgeous display of flowers standing in a vase in the middle of it. She inhaled the fresh blooms before picking up the list for the day.

It read:

Welcome! Cleaning supplies are in the janitorial closet off the kitchen.

*Main floor bathrooms (2)
*Vacuum formal living, library, and great room
*All windows/glass doors on main level
Thanks!

So she definitely wouldn't be seeing Jasper today. He'd probably stay on the second level—or were there three in this house?—every morning when she came. She navigated her way into the kitchen, which held the scent of food without any evidence of anyone being there to cook it. No pan sat on the stove. No dish rested in the sink. It was like someone had sprayed the scent of buttered toast and scrambled eggs into the air and then disappeared.

She wasn't entirely sure what a janitorial closet was. She lived in a one-bedroom condo only a block from the beach and only had two closets. One for jackets near the front door, and one in her bedroom. Though, while she opened one door and found mostly empty shelves, she supposed she had a linen closet too, if the floor-to-ceiling cabinet in the bathroom counted.

She closed the pantry door and tried the one next to it. That led to a mudroom, and another door that probably went into the garage.

The third door finally revealed what she was looking for. A bucket filled with cleaning supplies, brooms, mops, and vacuums in a variety of sizes, and several shelves with bottles of liquids and cans of powder.

Sasha decided to vacuum first, as it was a chore that she actually enjoyed. She could see the work being done, and she liked making perfectly straight lines in the carpet. As she pushed and pulled the vacuum over rugs in the library, and a light beige carpet in the formal living room, and a darker brown carpet in the great room, she yawned.

So she'd be tired. Didn't matter. This job would provide her with what she needed to keep her drink stand going and pay all her personal bills too.

She finished the windows and the bathrooms with only thirty minutes to spare, feeling sticky and sweaty despite the air conditioning filling the house. She wondered what on earth it would cost to heat or cool a place like this, once again glad she'd taken the job.

With her electricity out, she couldn't cool or heat her place, and she was at the mercy of Mother Nature. Not only that, but she hadn't had a hot shower in a week. With just enough time to spare before she had to leave to get to The Straw and get open for the day, she ran back out to her car and grabbed her bag.

She hadn't intended on showering at Jasper's place, but down at the recreation center like she'd toyed about doing for a solid week. But he was sure to have hot water, and she wouldn't be competing with all the morning lap swimmers.

And he won't even know, she told herself as she tiptoed back inside and cast a long look up the magnificent staircase to the second floor. She hadn't heard a peep from anyone or anything inside the house. Not a squeaky floorboard, not a phone ringing. Nothing. So he'd never know she'd used his shower. She'd be in and out in twenty minutes tops, ready for a long day making tropical drinks and smiling at tourists.

Sasha made sure to lock the door behind her, and she stood in the hot spray as relaxation coursed through her whole body. Though it had only been a week, she'd forgotten how wonderful and soothing hot water could be. She just had to get the electricity back on—and soon.

She towel-dried her hair and cracked the door two inches so the steam would filter out. She hated getting dressed in the same room where she'd showered, as if Hawaii needed more humidity than it already had.

Even with the cooler air from the hall coming in, her clothes still stuck to her as she pulled them on. She'd just loaded her toothbrush with minty paste when someone said, "Hello?" and the door drifted open to reveal a tall, broad, sandy-haired man standing there.

Jasper Rosequist.

Sasha sucked in a breath. Well, it was really a breath full of toothpaste and water, which caused her to choke.

And cough. And spit white foam everywhere, as if she were a freaking rabid dog.

"I'm sorry," he said, moving into the already too-tight space and pounding on her back. "I startled you. You okay?"

Of course she wasn't okay. The heat from his palm against her back sent shockwaves through her system, and he smelled like he'd just gotten out of the shower too. One where he'd lathered up with pine trees and warm apple cider.

Her eyes met his for a brief moment, and Sasha thought sure lightning would strike her. She managed to spit in the sink—*so attractive*, she thought—and take a drink of water to clear the evidence of rabies.

"I'm fine," she said, her voice much higher than it normally was. "Sorry, I was...." She glanced at her bag, where certain unmentionables were still visible.

She practically dove onto the bag to conceal them, and when she looked at Jasper again, he'd backed to the doorway. He had to be perfect, of course, wearing a pair of pressed black slacks and a polo the color of the sky on a perfect summer day. If he put on a suit coat jacket, he'd be a twin to Newton, the last man who'd made her heart try to fling itself free of her body.

"You showered here?" he asked.

"I, uh...." Sasha didn't know what to say, and her pulse pounded now for an entirely different reason. This man had no idea what her life was like, and he'd *never* understand unless he had to live without hot water. Or air conditioning. Or the ability to keep food cold.

"Yes," she finally said, deciding to own it. Maybe she could still get paid for the cleaning she'd done that morning. "I showered here. I had a few minutes before my next job, and I was kind of gross from all the cleaning. It won't happen again." She gazed evenly at him, telling herself that he wasn't more important than her just because he had money and she didn't.

He said nothing for so long that Sasha's nerves started to fray. "Are you going to fire me?" she asked, lifting her chin and hoping with everything she had that he'd say no.

He just stood there, mute and growing more attractive by the moment as she took in the ripple of his muscles under his shirtsleeves and across his chest, the way his hair spiked in the front like he was trying to be the lead singer of a boy band, and the way he stood as if he knew he'd be able to charm her into doing whatever he wanted.

What was wrong with him? Sasha still needed to put on makeup and get over to The Straw, and with every second he stood there staring with those dark green eyes was another second she'd be late. So whether she found him attractive or not, she needed to break this guy out of whatever trance he'd fallen into. Stat.

———

Read STRAW AND DIAMONDS, the next book in the Getaway Bay Resort series, and go with Sasha and Jasper as they find their island happily-ever-after—with diamonds!

BOOKS IN THE GETAWAY BAY RESORT ROMANCE SERIES

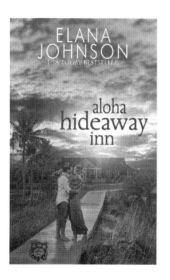

Aloha Hideaway Inn (Book 1): Can Stacey and the Aloha Hideaway Inn survive strange summer weather, the arrival of the new resort, *and* the start of a special relationship?

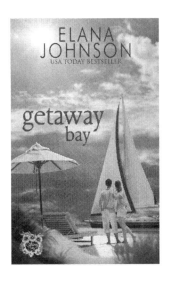

Getaway Bay (Book 2): Can Esther deal with dozens of business tasks, unhappy tourists, *and* the twists and turns in her new relationship?

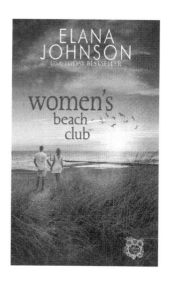

Women's Beach Club (Book 3):
With the help of her friends in the Beach Club, can Tawny solve the mystery, stay safe, and keep her man?

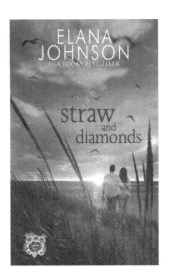

Straw and Diamonds (Book 4): Can Sasha maintain her sanity amidst their busy schedules, her issues with men like Jasper, and her desires to take her business to the next level?

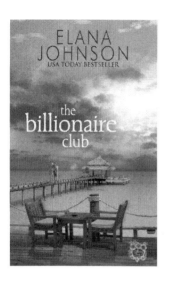

The Billionaire Club (Book 5): Can Lexie keep her business affairs in the shadows while she brings her relationship out of them? Or will she have to confess everything to her new friends...and Jason?

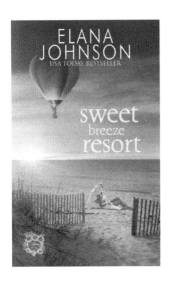

Sweet Breeze Resort (Book 6): Can Gina manage her business across the sea and finish the remodel at Sweet Breeze, all while developing a meaningful relationship with Owen and his sons?

Rainforest Retreat (Book 7): As their paths continue to cross and Lawrence and Maizee spend more and more time together, will he find in her a retreat from all the family pressure? Can Maizee manage her relationship with her boss, or will she once again put her heart—and her job—on the line?

Getaway Bay Singles (Book 8): Can Katie bring him into her life, her daughter's life, and manage her business while he manages the app? Or will everything fall apart for a second time?

Turn the page to view series starters from three of my other series!

BOOKS IN THE STRANDED IN GETAWAY BAY ROMANCE SERIES

Meet the McLaughlin Sisters in Getaway Bay as they encounter disaster after disaster...including the men they get stranded with. From ex-boyfriends to cowboys to football stars, these sisters can bring any man to his knees when the cards are stacked against them.

The Perfect Storm (Book 1): A freak storm has her sliding down the mountain...right into the arms of her ex. As Eden and Holden spend time out in the wilds of Hawaii trying to survive, their old flame is rekindled. But with secrets and old feelings in the way, will Holden be able to take all the broken pieces of his life and put them back together in a way that makes sense? Or will he lose his heart and the reputation of his company because of a single landslide?

BOOKS IN THE GETAWAY BAY ROMANCE SERIES

Escape to Getaway Bay and meet your new best friends as these women navigate their careers, their love lives, and their own dreams and desires. Each heartwarming love story shows the power of women in their own lives and the lives of their friends.

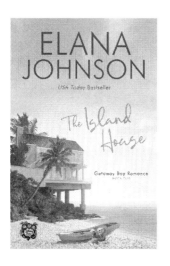

The Island House (Book 1): Charlotte Madsen's whole world came crashing down six months ago with the words, "I met someone else."

Can Charlotte navigate the healing process to find love again?

BOOKS IN THE HILTON HEAD ROMANCE SERIES

Visit the South Carolina Lowcountry and picturesque Hilton Head Island in this sweet women's fiction romance series by USA Today bestselling author, Elana Johnson.

The Love List (Hilton Head Romance, Book 1): Bea turns to her lists when things get confusing and her love list morphs once again... Can she add *fall in love at age 45* to the list and check it off?

ABOUT ELANA

Elana Johnson is the USA Today bestselling and Kindle
All-Star author of dozens of clean and wholesome
contemporary romance novels. She lives in Utah, where
she mothers two fur babies, works with her husband full-
time, and eats a lot of veggies while writing. Find her on
her website at feelgoodfictionbooks.com

Made in the USA
Middletown, DE
01 August 2024

58335633R00146